2010

MW01140953

Garden of Eden

To Lady Di
A South High Beauty
born in God's Country

Love

LARRY HENRY

McAnally Flats Press
PO Box 1058
Louisville, TN 37777
www.McAnallyFlatsPress.com

LCCN: 2008944396
ISBN-10 0-9819209-0-X
ISBN-13 978-0-9819209-0-0
Copyright: TXu 1-576-119

Cover Design and Interior Art: Cory Mollenhour, CM Design
Interior Design: J. L. Saloff
Typography: Minion Pro, Bordeaux Roman Bold

v.. 1.0
First Edition, 2009
Printed on acid free paper.

This Book Is Dedicated to
The Loving Memory of My Parents:

Mildred Geneva Butler Henry
Hugh Jackson (Jay) Henry III

And The Armed Forces of The United States of America

God Bless America

Chapter One

Young High School

John & Bubba

John Henry Jackson was waiting on tomorrow. So was Robert Barthalamaeus (Bubba) Smith. That tomorrow never walked up and banged on the front door gave them comfort. An adopted sense of well-being. Affinity with a redoubtable destiny they often dreamt of but had yet to transform into anything resembling success. Being on hold gave them an alibi. Their stage-managed *hors de combat*. That grand analogy for making Cs while chasing hog-wild after tender poontang all over The University of Tennessee campus. Their nebulous intersection for self-serving license to turn left on red, meaning they didn't work and lived off dear ole mom and dad. The American dream come home to roost.

Yet, they were the future, these capsized heroes of the Southern Circle Drive-In Restaurant. The future bedrock of Western Democracy. America's secret weapon against Karl Marx and Poppa Joe Stalin.

More to the point, they were residents in the Knox County lockup, again, for the second time in six weeks.

Bubba opened a pair of bloodshot eyes. His world tilted, then derailed off the cliff. Shit-ugly and venomously twisted. He didn't recognize exactly where he was just yet and for a moment he felt deranged and somehow violated.

He found himself facedown atop a smelly mattress. A jail bed. The thing was held together by metal struts on forty-five degree angles to a steel frame painted gray. The same color as the cinder block wall behind it, reminding Bubba of fungus and the foul cigarette taste in his mouth. He rolled over painfully, setting off new rounds of depth charges inside his splitting head. Above him he saw the grim underside of more of the same. The opposite wall was a duplicate of its evil twin but the double bunk over there was empty.

John was flat on his back on the floor asleep. His mattress was reinforced concrete with a drain in the middle. The ceiling more or less matched John's Bohemian pallet, minus the drain. Rivet heads the size of nickels secured the slender beams and metal struts. Concrete cinder blocks, more fungus gray, made up the rear bulkhead wall, offset by a dirty toilet arrangement, almost white, centered with no seat. No toilet paper, old newspapers served that function, no sink, no pillows, no cigar. One-inch steel bars stood out as grim reminders of Bubba's unholy whereabouts, complimented by a manifold steel door of exacting proportions. The taxpayer's ambiance was Early Industrial.

Bubba closed his eyes against his claustrophobic accommodations. The pain in his head resembled galloping China Syndrome. Being nineteen, he mused, was no walk in the park. Too many uncertainties, too much…insecurity…too many…nothing made sense. Too much…damn it…whatever the hell. Then it began to take shape inside his whiskey-laden noggin….Question Marks! Some…it seemed…just sprang up like weeds. Others…fell out of the sky like bird squeeze. The big ones sprouted out his ears like daisies.

Most mornings, he deciphered with piss-elegant clarity, he crawled out of bed and whizzed a yellow stream of the little bastards down the john. Brushing his teeth, he envisioned a big black one stamped on his forehead in the bathroom mirror. At the breakfast table he ate the tasty things with orange juice and coffee, buttered toast and preserves, prepared by his doting mother on fake china plates, ringed around the edges with scrollwork and tiny blue flowers, and stamped on the bottom with Made In Japan. The apron Mom wore had intricate little pink ones embroidered across the front.

His two younger sisters had the same "I Don't Get It" lipsticked across their foreheads. Virgin distress signals lettered in Old English. But his dad had none. Not one. No ship laden with troubled cargo was this confident individual. Bubba wished he could be more like his father for the simple reason Pop always knew where he was going. Bubba hadn't a clue about his future destination or how to go about getting under way. Or even where to buy a ticket.

Bubba had determined some time ago that John was no Sam Catchem in the What Does It All Mean Department his damn self. Their garish routine consisted of intractable hours spent in class, campus parking violations, hanging out at the Southern Circle Drive-In Restaurant, drag racing the family automobiles, and chauvinistic outbursts of the male pecking order in various beer joints and other drive-in restaurants around town. Uncle Andy's Greek restaurant on Cumberland Avenue, Sigma Phi Epsilon blowouts, the Brown Derby on Kingston Pike, Big Orange football, Comer's Sports Center downtown, and bootleg whiskey and the dry heaves. Siphoning gasoline from parked cars, dancing at the Carnival Club 'til two in the morning, the Pink Pony in Vestal, and pumping iron at John Paschal's health club. To add to the melodrama, there was Bill's Barn in West Knoxville, copping speed to study all night, skipping class, the Tic Toc on Magnolia Avenue, searching high and low for more "diet pills," lying to their parents about damn near everything, and spinning their wheels center stage in woebegone hormonal teenage frustration.

Robert was searching for the answers. His was a serious disposition he kept hidden from everyone, especially John. He didn't under-stand why the older generation carried on so about these being the best years of their lives. Why did he feel so insecure and confused all the time? What about his future career? What career? He noted similar dysfunctions in other teens his age, John more so than anyone else. If these were their best years, God help them by the time they reached thirty. Forty seemed too distant to even contemplate. It didn't make sense to Bubba, which was precisely the reason he projected so much youthful uncertainty.

A minor commotion out front signaled feeding time. Bubba rec-ognized the squeaking of the wheels on the breakfast trolley. He rolled over gingerly and sat up. His lower lip was split. Then he noticed the blood caked down the front of his new shirt. Slowly, last night's mis-adventure began to unwind like a B-grade movie. He wanted to shout "cut," but the phantoms of guilt came gliding forth anyway. That guy in the new Chevy giving John a ration of shit after John accidentally scraped the paint on the dude's door. Bubba threw his French fries on the prissy bastard. That didn't sit too well with his three buddies, so the whole car emptied out. Then John smashed a beer bottle over the big one's head. That just pissed him off worse, so he blasted Bubba square in the chops. He remembered nearly going down. A kick to the gonads slowed down Godzilla, but the skinny driver nailed his ass with a haymaker to the jaw. He remembered lots of stars and seeing John swinging a tire iron. Bubba was throwing punches like Marlon Brando in The Wild One and generally getting his ass kicked. Then the cops pulled up and everyone ran except the two drunks.

"Hey, asshole. Time for breakfast."

John stirred on the dirty floor. "Fuck you."

"Wake up, shit-for-brains. They're comin' down the hall."

"I ain't hungry. You eat it."

Bubba positioned himself beside the heavy door.

"OK…shit!" John pulled himself erect, stared red-eyed at Bubba, the floor, red-eyed at Bubba, then sat down miserably on the bottom tier of his bunk. "Ohhhh, God," he moaned. John was pregnant with hangover and a bloody nose.

"You look like shit."

John lurched to his feet, still half drunk, fishing for a cigarette. "I resemble that remark. What's so important about jail food anyway?"

"Breakfast is the main meal of the day. Keeps you healthy, man."

"Sounds reasonable. Guess if I eat this cuisine it'll make me be a big star like you, huh? Where are we anyway?"

"County jail, same as last time."

"That's great. I knew this was gonna happen. Locked up in the Black Hole of Calcutta with a sick fucker about to go crazy talkin' 'bout breakfast food. You gonna try and fuck me too, ain'cha? Damn, my head hurts."

Bubba giggled, minced a step sideways holding onto the bars, snickered again, glanced over at his woebegone friend, then flooded the cell with great peals of laughter. Helplessly he clung to the bars and howled. John fell back on the bed holding his sides in pained hysterics as tears puddled up from ruptured plumbing.

"Shut up in there!" The turnkey was not amused. "You idjits want breakfast or not?"

New outbursts of laughter assaulted the bare-bulb atmosphere. John pounded the mattress with both hands. "No!" he blurted out.

"Yes, sir! Yes, we do!" Bubba was hungry. "Don't pay no attention to him. He's a drunk crazy person. Runs in the family. You know how they get."

"Un-huh. If they're like you two idjits, the nuts is winnin'." A metal tray and cup were passed through the rectangular slot in the door.

"Fried bologna an' grits! Thank ya, mazzuh, thank ya. Next time we wants possum an' sweet taters."

John hooted gleefully, silently clapping his hands. The trusty cook, circa Gabby Hayes, heehawed a toothless shriek, rolled his yellow eyes at Bubba, then cut a resounding whiskey fart. Bubba pantomimed Chuck Berry's duck walk back to his bunk, carefully holding his steaming tray. Finally, he cackled. The curmudgeon jailer flashed a tobacco-stained grin at the old dipso who, in comic appreciation, fired another 100 proof salvo.

As they began to roll away, John lurched up to the bars. His dormant appetite had gained its footing. "Sir, wait…what about me?"

Another tray and cup were birthed through the metal womb and John retired to his side of their delivery quarters. Soon the tray was spotless, mopped and polished to a dull finish by a final slab of white Merita bread. Across the cell Bubba sat up in bed with his back against the wall, savoring every morsel as though he were dining on Maine lobster at the Regas Restaurant. He was oblivious to John's inquiring stare. The crotch of Bubba's jeans and his torn windbreaker were splattered with last night's bloody misdemeanor.

"I sure do owe ya one" John said.

"You was pretty messed up." Bubba grinned.

"Hell, I was shit-faced." John fingered a newfound lump above his left ear. "What about that big mother? Looked like he was givin' you your money's worth, all right."

"Damn, I reckon. I busted him a good one two or three times but he just kept on comin'. Might be a good thing your cop buddies showed up when they did. I might a hurt that feller." The top three buttons of Bubba's shirt were missing.

"No way, ole buddy. I'd a worked my way 'round to that big bastard sooner or later."

Bubba wondered to himself if maybe his best friend really did have a drinking problem. Sometimes when John drank too much he became wild and just plain mean. Like last night with that tire iron. But he did the same thing when he punched the driver in the face. What a pair, he thought. Sipping the last of his black coffee, he thought again about the Marine Corps and Parris Island.

By ten-thirty they were back on the streets. Orbit had posted their bond by bartering with the bail bondsman, using the title to his automobile as collateral. They called him Orbit because Tommy Cameron orbited the drive-in restaurants looking for cute girls to park beside. Parking beside pretty women was as far as the Vestal Casanova had yet advanced regarding his curiosity over the mysterious opposite sex.

Facing a new day with a plutonium hangover wasn't exactly a patriotic accolade following the breakfast of champions, but the curmudgeon had released them anyway. American jurisprudence was an exacting science. Sometimes the guilty were set free to protect the innocent.

Chapter Two

Chapman Highway

Red's Dilemma

Orbit was a UT frat-rat freshman, all As in all subjects, an aficionado of science fiction tales of adventure, and a mental practitioner of Walter Mitty. The small five-foot-seven-inch scholar wore a red James Dean windbreaker and drove a 1957 red Chevrolet Bel Air convertible. He and John had a physical education class together. Orbit had come to dislike phys ed because the bigger boys made fun of him. John became his friend the day he told Orbit about the Charles Atlas bodybuilding course.

He and John were parked at the Southern Circle Drive-In Restaurant beside Bubba and Bubba's cousin Red, who was a senior running back at South High School. Red's girlfriend, Carolyn Harris, had just dumped him the week before, with nary a howdy do, for a fellow classmate that played flute in the South High Band.

"So then she says I ain't got no couth! Like, I thought she meant some damn thing about the way I dress or something. Well, shit! So, after our big fight, I go home and look it up. Why I got more couth than that jerk. More! I got couth, man."

Carolyn's pretty face stared back at him through the austere cracks of reality, reminding him in vain of naked glories past.

"Your problem isn't couth, ole buddy. What you need is some gimmick to make Carolyn think she's missing the boat." Orbit's genius was thought-provoking.

John liked it. "Say, that's right. You need an angle, something to turn her on. Make her socks run up and down like window shades, but what?"

Orbit leaned forward, looking over at Bubba. "He's your family. What tawdry secrets you hiding over there?"

"Danged if I know." He reached up to scratch his chin. "He's a good ball player. Good hell-raiser too. Got kicked outta the Deuces for fighting. Remember that one, dude?"

Red smiled, nodding his head.

Bubba stared out the window trying to conjure a solution for his cousin's dilemma. "Mother's a hairdresser. Old man paints houses. Sister's a damn hippie."

Red punched Bubba's arm. Bubba's eyes were slightly glazed from too much bourbon and Coke. "Why not kill the bitch and burn 'er house down?"

Everyone laughed except Red. "Come on, guys, this ain't funny, OK?"

Alcohol and logic mix in a similar fashion as hard-shelled Baptists and ladies of the evening. An hour later the four intellects had landed in their cups, care of the bootleg express. Poor Red was beginning to resemble a lonesome cowpoke who'd lost his pony along the Chisholm Trail. He, too, had whiskey whistling out both ears.

"Well, just fuck it! Why don't you catch 'im out an' just coldcock 'is ass an get 'er done? That's what I'd do fer some flute weasel playin' 'round in my bid'ness." John was animated. "I don't git all this talk.

What's the big deal here, anyway?"

"Maybe she just likes 'em bigger. You a short-stroker, Red? I hear they're doin' implants down at the hospital. Maybe you better go on down an' get some broom handle or garden hose sewed in. Carolyn finds out, she'll be over there at your house scratchin' up the yard an' howlin' at tha moon. You'll have to beat 'er off with a damn pole."

Bubba had seized on the vicarious humor associated with his cousin's woebegone misery. He found it amusing, the thought of Red getting his emotions caught in his fly. But the idea of Carolyn humping Flute Weasel was breaking poor Red's intoxicated heart.

John savored the thought of calling up for a dick appointment with good Doctor Pinocchio. Surely Delta Delta Delta would hurl themselves at his feet with carnal screams and giggles.

Orbit was seeing double. His preoccupation was remembering a past gangbang at his fraternity house .

"Sure, an' cheerleaders too!" Bubba added. "They'll be jumpin' outta trees, sneakin' in the locker room, trippin' yer ass tryin' ta jump under ya. Boy howdy! I could use somma that all right. How 'bout it, Orb? You wanna get rotor-rootered?"

Orbit snickered drunkenly. "Lord, yes, long's I don't git them crabs. Happened last time, ya know. Ever' body at the frat house got 'em 'cept me. Brother McVay brought his date to this party, see. Then he passes out and she takes on ever' body don't have a date. Some with dates too. He didn't find out, though. I couldn't believe it. Anyway, we like ta never got rid a them crabs." Orbit concealed the unhappy fact that he did not participate due to his humiliating shyness with females. His carnal experience to date was Miss Thumb and her four sisters.

The fifth was passed around until only a swallow remained in the bottom, rendering the topic under discussion into a rambling dissertation on the merits of pussy. Their frontal lobes gurgled and constricted due to mutual grease fires of the brain. Finally, poor Red could stand it no longer.

"Fuck your stupid fraternity! An' fuck this bullshit!" He jerked out of the car, slamming the door with a final bang. "An' fuck all you!" Trembling with pubescent rage fueled by too much Early Times, he strode away toward the alley behind the restaurant.

Bubba jumped out, fell crazily onto the asphalt, then ran after his rapidly disappearing cousin. "Hey, I'm sorry. We didn't mean nothin'. Come on, Red, I'm sorry, really. We'll figure somethin' out. Red, wait!"

Red stopped dead still then turned around in the stance of a boxer. Bubba saw the hurt in the his cousin's eyes. He saw something else too that made him wince with pain.

"Big college deals. You don't know shit. My daddy can't send me, an' I ain't gettin' no football scholarship. I'm too little. Nobody wants me. So where does that leave ole Red? Be a house painter like my old man? Sell fuckin' used cars? What the hell do I have to offer Carolyn? You don't know what it's like, man." Red began to cry.

"Awww, God, don't do that. I didn't mean it." Bubba was horrified at being the cause of his cousin's tears. He, in turn, found cinders in his own 86 proof vision. "Jesus, Red, I'm sorry as shit, man." Two big ones rolled down his cheeks and fell off his chin.

Orbit and John wandered onto the grassy knoll behind the parked automobiles and into the back alley where the two cousins were both sniffling and taking a leak. They felt as bad as Bubba for their mortal breech of drinking etiquette among drinking buddies.

"Gosh, old buddy, we didn't mean to hurt yer feelings none. Orbit here's drunk as a coot. Me too, I reckon. By God, we all are."

Red smiled sheepishly, wiping his nose with the back of his sleeve.

Bubba craned himself up to his full agenda of six feet two, hand on his chest, solemnly proclaiming, "No more bullshit!"

John placed his hand over his heart. "No more bullshit!"

Orbit's hand bumped his nose, finally locating his chest. "No more bullshit!"

"I apologize for losin' my couth," Red replied.

"This calls for another bottle of the grape," hooted Orbit.

"Damn right!" echoed the Three Musketeers.

A second trip to Vestal produced another boisterous fifth of loud mouth. By midnight all four of them were blood brothers for life. Red and Bubba drank themselves stupid in toasts to brotherhood and comradeship. Finally, the carhop cut off their setups fearing they'd kill themselves driving home. John and Orbit were in slightly better condition, but both were slowly painting themselves into a corner over the fickle departure of one Miss Carolyn Harris.

"I ain't sure 'bout this." Orbit was the intellectual skeptic.

"I tell ya it's in a book." John was the closet romantic.

"What book?" Orbit was lukewarm to the idea, but chicken shit.

"I fergit. Ayn Rand wrote it. But this dude sets the oil wells on fire and the chicks all dig it an' he's a big hero and they all screw his brains out. That's all I know."

"Jesus!"

"I don't remember that part."

"Sounds like somethin' outta the Klan manual."

"We'll be careful, OK?"

"They won't find us for weeks."

"How 'bout it Red? It's yer show."

"Far out…let's do 'er."

"OK, Bubba?"

"If my buddy Red's fer it, I am my damn self."

"Orbit?"

"Jesus!"

"Damn it, Orbit!"

"All right, but you gotta drive."

"No sweat, let's get the stuff."

John piloted Orbit's intoxicated convertible out Chapman Highway until it swung hard right onto Larry Drive. They decelerated down the street until it leveled out in the flat beside a long gravel driveway. John killed the engine, and silence. The neighborhood was asleep. A mesmeric world appeared before them, suggesting illumination from beneath the earth's surface with its stark white glow from the moon. The Four Horsemen gazed in wonder at their alien landscape.

At the top of the driveway crouched an impregnable Southern fortress. Its Perma-Stone walls reflected the cold gray color of moon rock. Ghosts of legions past dwelt there. Tall sentinels guarding the mysterious structure pointed their fingered boughs in tribute toward the heavens. A silent breeze stirred the ground leaves, recalling gray images of dangers long ago. Scattered patches of shadow lay among the secret hiding places. It was John's house. Something dark dipped past the windshield.

"Gaaaa…did you see that?" Orbit was spooked.

"Whoa! What tha hell!" Red leaned halfway over the front seat, staring up at the thing bobbing and weaving above them.

Bubba twisted around sideways, looking up from his car door windowsill.

"Cool it, will ya. It's just a ole bat." John laughed. "I'd hate to meet up with something god-awful with you freaks around."

"I ain't never seen no bat cuttin' no didos before."

"It was lookin' in here!"

"Y'all hush or you'll wake up the whole place. I'll be back in a minute."

John cut a trail up the driveway, keeping well over in the grass to avoid making noise in the gravel. A cloud passed over the moon. It was difficult to see without the lunar body lighting the way. Just as quickly it reappeared, blinding him momentarily. The garage was straight ahead so he made for the two black rectangles at the end of the house.

The blow was swift and brutal, causing him to cry out in fear and pain. Stars danced gaily before his startled eyes as he reeled away from his unseen assailant, fists in the fighting position. It landed in the leaves right beside him with a thump. Again he startled wildly, hurling himself sideways for escape into a hickory tree. The stars were breeding that night. Then he saw the rake he had forgotten and left in the yard.

"Son of a bitch!"

The villain was dispatched with a vicious kick, gouging an inch-long slab of skin off his ankle.

"You Fuck!"

His frustration swelled to heroic abundance. With tears smarting from both eyes and blood leaking from his upper lip, John stormed across the parking area, disappearing into the maw of the welcome darkness. Moments later he emerged, carrying a five-gallon can by the handle, and ran down the driveway. A light across the street came on as he yanked open the car door.

"Here, sit this in the floor. Kill that cigarette, Bubba."

"It's sure big enough. It's full too."

"Say, what happened to you?"

"I stepped on the damn rake."

All three of them stared at John's bleeding mouth in the door lights, then burst out laughing. Orbit regained himself as another light came on across the street.

"You better get us outta here."

"You got it."

John gunned the engine and roared away in a cloud of dust and burning rubber. Their mission of mayhem and mercy was under way.

Traffic had thinned to singles and deuces as they retraced their earlier journey, drawn yet again toward the magnetic attraction of the Southern Circle Drive-In and a date with destiny. Their faithful steed transported them to a place in the shadows behind Jimmy's Esso at the intersection of Chapman Highway and Young High Pike. A rejected automobile tire was soon located and jammed upright in the back seat between Red's knees. Off they roared again to display Red's misbetrothed affections to a member of that other half of their species, which none of them understood any better than Chinese arithmetic or the solar winds.

Red envisioned his anesthetized self as the tush-hog conquistador navigating the treacherous coral reefs through the uncharted waters of the South High Band. Coming about full sail, his boarding party armed and ready. For Love and Glory! Febrile wish-dreams with kudzued determination, and hoped for lust in Carolyn's cobalt blue eyes. Will she strike her colors freely with labored breath and gentle persuasion? Or must he broadside the Pirate Queen?

> *Dear Teenage Father,*
>
> *Deliver unto these slack-minded mortals those cool, clear evenings for the big high school football event, that delectable fresh aroma of new-mown grass, those marvelous autumn hot dogs with pickle relish and sweet Vidalia onions, and the bountiful wonder of sock hops while wearing no footwear. Grant them golden memories amid the merry-go-round of youth. Let them always remember and happily rejoice in this fleeting repass before an unfamiliar dawn, which beckons with false promise and surreptitious intent to question-eyed youngsters whose genes smolder in the night. Grant them safe harbor, blessed Father. Let them blossom as leaders among their own kind, not as plastic doorstops for ambition-driven toad masters.*
>
> *Will she kiss him before the big game? Imagined forgiveness and that salt-sweet nectar of reunion? Oh, yes, please, dear Teenage Father. With perfumed hair and defrocked shoulders beneath those golden harvest moons above their*

drive-in Xanadu. Succulent peach mounds and fuzzy silken treasures. Society's forbidden fruit orbiting that grand parade of immortality on a conjugal front seat in the very back row, wrapped for delivery in the anthracite blanket of nocturne. Forever longed for…those magnificent dreams of tomorrow, and the sweet velvet mystery of sex. Oh, glorious halls and rightly wicked, these Halls of Common.

World without end. Amen.

"This is killer," exclaimed Red. "She'll flip out."

"So will most of the neighbors," observed Orbit.

"My girl's gonna be the talk uh South High School."

"Flute Weasel can't top this." John was supremely confident.

"We'll be lucky if we don't land on the chain gang for burning down the neighborhood."

"Orbit…this one's for love!"

John winked hugely in the rearview mirror at Red in the back seat, then looked over at Bubba who was fast asleep. He smiled to himself with affection for his big friend. John had sobered somewhat so driving was less of a chore now.

The quest took them down Moody Avenue, which turned into Sevierville Pike past Woodlawn, then left on Sevier and right on Allen. And there it was. The 900-square-foot mansion of the vaunted Miss Harris. Similar plantations faced both sides of the street.

Red was beside himself being this close to his imagined High School Princess.

Something appeared in the back of John's mind trying to warn him away, but he closed the door.

"Wake up, Bubba."

Bubba opened his eyes as they rolled to a halt some little distance past the house beneath the shaded limbs of a persimmon tree.

John assumed command. "You guys ready?" he whispered. Six round eyes responded with approved nods of conspiracy. "Come on, then."

Four skulking figures emerged from the dark of the persimmon tree, carrying a punctured 6-70/15 Goodyear tire, a five-gallon can of Esso regular, and the half-baked notion of transmogrified deliverance. Red extracted a box of King Edward matches from his faded blue jeans while Orbit and Bubba positioned the tire in front of the house in the middle of Allen Avenue. John hurriedly followed along behind them splashing gasoline inside the automobile tire and up and down the roadway for several yards.

"You're on." John nodded.

Red stepped forward as the others fled to the safety of the convertible. Holding two matches between his thumb and his forefinger, he leaned forward and struck the matches.

WHOOOMP!!!

Fire flashed between his legs and all around him as the ground-laden fumes ignited outward, sending a fireball skyward half the size of the house. For an instant the billowing flames behind him and the lesser ones licking around his calves gave Red the stranded silhouette of a man knee-deep in hell. He became all elbows and knees, dancing a smoking jig to the car, slapping wildly at his hair and clothing en route. The tire caught fire and began to burn with hollow crackling sounds, releasing a cumulous black cloud mixed with leaping yellow flames.

"Hey, you! Stop!"

John dropped the shift into low and roared away with no lights. The moon was light enough. Red had lost his eyelashes and some of his hair, but the conquistador from South High School wore the weird smile of a man who had just found his rhythm.

Chapter Three

Southern Circle

The Stone Quarry

They were parked at the Southern Circle Drive-In Restaurant on Chapman Highway. The Southern Circle was situated one block north of Young High School. This was the 20th century's belle époque for South Knoxville, and the popular hangout for Young High School students and local area residents. Some discovered their destinies there. Their rights of passage. It was a gay and festive atmosphere. Teens got out of their automobiles, talking and laughing, meeting friends and making new acquaintances. Some encountered their soul mates. Others met up with Johnny Law.

Babe Maloy's was another asphalt carousel of teenage intrigue a mile farther north toward town. South High School students congregated at Babe's. The majority soon became acquainted with alcohol and tobacco, while forming a host of lasting relationships. These unique places to park one's wheels, then order fries and a Coke brought to their cars, represented their drive-in country clubs.

Their discussion had been in progress about thirty minutes and appeared to be slipping through the cracks for John and the boys. The beer was all gone too. Suzie, the local gangbang specialist, was in a coy mood tonight. She was proving to them via the bearded clam between her shapely thighs just what the 1960s version of an early feminist was all about. Orbit, the only virgin still intact in the group, was about to wet his pants for fear Suzie wouldn't deliver the poontang. The whole entourage was aghast with raging hormones.

"I don't know. Four of ya sounds like an awful lot to me. I don't think I oughta."

"Look, babe, four ain't too many. It's the astrological perfect number. Hey, come on now. Damn! I promise. You'll have a great time. Me an Orbit an ole Red. And Bubba! That big, good-looking dude. Wha'cha got to lose?"

"What if somebody finds out? I could get kicked outta school, ya know."

"Who's to tell? We sure as hell ain't. Tell ya what. Let's all go down to Abner's and get ourselves a fifth and have a big party! It's a swell night and we got the radio an' all. It'll be killer, Suzie."

"Well, I don't know. Four of ya sounds like too many. What kinda fifth?"

"Vodka, whiskey, rum…anything you want. Come on, be a sport. We'll have a big time. Besides, tomorrow is Saturday and you can sleep all day."

"A lot you know about it. My daddy has me up cleanin' the house, cookin' for him and my brothers and sisters, shoppin' groceries. Besides, you probably say this stuff to all the girls, don't you, John? You do, don't you?"

"No way! I ain't blowin' smoke, Suzie."

"Sure you do. You blow more smoke than a fireplace, Johnny."

"Hey, I ain't never lied to you. No way." John was somewhat hurt by Suzie's casual remark. Nor was this his first encounter with Suzie in a gangbang.

"I know, honey. I'm just givin' ya a hard time. Sorta like the hard one you'd like to give me, maybe."

"Let's do 'er. Let's go party. Orbit ain't never been with a woman before. You'll be savin' the lad from a fate worse than death. Whadaya say? Come on, honey. Purty please with sugar on it?"

"Golly, four dudes at one time. And Orbit a virgin. I might go if they got gin. You promise none of ya won't tell nobody?"

"Not nobody, babe! I swear. No way, Suz. Cross my heart and hope to die!"

All four gentlemen were elated with various stages of precoital anxiety. Four semi-intoxicated Volunteers intent on a mission of mercy. Said mission, of course, being to bury their Wiener schnitzels up to the pubic hilt in the flat-bellied love canal of the hottest Hose Queen between downtown Gay Street and the Horne Drive-In Theatre out Chapman Highway toward Seymour. Saint Suzie of the Sacred Order of the Ole In-Out.

Orbit nearly swooned with the prospect of getting laid. At the same time he was scared out of his wits. Suzie was a tall, attractive eighteen-year-old beauty with long auburn hair, baby blue eyes, and a pair of knockers that would make the Pope do a double take. She hailed from a poor blue-collar family living in Vestal. Her devout Baptist mother died from cancer of the lungs when she was fourteen. She being the oldest, responsibility for the household chores passed down to her.

Her thirty-nine-year-old daddy worked as a marble cutter for Candora Marble Company in Vestal. Tall and handsome, rugged and muscular, he'd turned to the Good Book following the passing of his beautiful wife, Esther. Suzie was the spitting image of her deceased mother.

The circuit rider passed through town once every spring and again each fall, always in two old Army trucks driven by him and his prodigal offspring. There they settled in the poorest sections of Knoxville, asking the pastors in the poor sections to send men over to put up the revival tent and set out the 2 x 12 x 16 wooden planks on twelve-inch cinder blocks, which served as seats for the multitudes of sinners. Each man was paid with a pint of moonshine and four one-dollar bills. The circuit rider's brother in Kentucky made the pop skull, so their expenses were held to a minimum. Reverend Ichabod was quite familiar with the wickedness of his fellow travelers for Glory, so he sold the brew out back following each night's sermon at four bucks a bottle.

Son David was a devout preacher of the gospel, especially in the company of pretty young women. He often anointed them with 120 proof libations, flavored with Orange Crush or Grapette Soda. Many an intoxicated female found her deliverance beneath the lusting loins of good Son David.

Suzie had discovered her deliverance in the backend of one of the Army trucks while the kids and Daddy Brown were inside the Amee Semple MePherson hoedown, delivering up his hard-earned currency to good Reverend Ichabod. Everybody was singing up a storm.

> "Throw out the lifeline! Throw out the lifeline!
> Someone is drifting away;
> Throw out the lifeline! Throw out the lifeline!
> Someone is sinking today."

Son David had his sleeping quarters in back of the truck, complete with mattress and an ice cooler stocked with cold cuts and white lightning. Half a pint later, Miss Suzie took her seat on the Moonbeam Express, where Son David initiated his ritualistic boom-bobba-boom-bobba-boom, complete with "Hallelujahs" and "Oh, my God!" This went on for three nights running until the circuit rider loaded up his tent, his Bible, and good Son David, then set sail for his next batch of gullible Christians west on Highway 62 over in Wartburg, Tennessee.

The sexual union between good Son David and herself had awakened in Suzie a sexual awareness, an unbridled appetite she didn't understand. Suzie hated being poor but loved sex. Sometimes it frightened her. But more often than not she gave in to the fire down below. She wondered if God would punish her for her carnal sins. Sundays, she walked her younger brothers and sisters to the little church on Avenue A. Suzie prayed to God for a rich husband like Pat Boone or Paul Newman. She also prayed for a place in Heaven for all their souls. Suzie's heart was in the right place, looking after her family. She was a senior at Young High School. Having sex with the college boys from "better homes" was her notion of social climbing.

They departed the Southern Circle in a raucous mood, arriving at Abner Johnson's bootleg emporium with Orbit and Suzie lodged strategically on the back seat. Red, Bubba, and John rode up front with John driving. A tough looking hombre with pale skin and a dark mustache was sitting on the back porch smoking a cigarette when they pulled up. The house was a white two-story affair with clapboard siding. Across the half-moon driveway behind the house sat a white cinder block building with a flat roof. The front door hung open for ventilation, revealing a lonesome light bulb dangling nooselike from a pine plank ceiling, medalled with blackened cobwebs in a smoke-cured room.

A full compliment of strays were seated around a green felt card table playing six-card stud poker. John recognized one of them as a deacon from his church. Beyond the gamblers was a second room closed off by a heavy frame door painted orange. A rectangular slot had been whittled in the second panel from the top of the orange door. The money room. Tall oaks and maples sheltered the two buildings on both sides of the driveway.

The screen door to the back porch screeched open, then banged shut.

"Howdy. What can I do fer you folks?"

"Ya got any gin?" John asked.

"Well, we got Seagram's and Gilbey's." The hombre leaned down to

see inside the car. He appraised the situation quickly. Suzie had been
there before.

"How much is a fifth?"

"Five bucks. Just come in last night."

"Tell him Seagram's." Suzie was enthusiastic about the gin.

"Yeah, Seagram's," Orbit replied from the back seat.

All of them were enthusiastic about Suzie, even the hombre was
taken with her ample charms.

"I guess we'll have the Seagram's, then."

"We got quarts fer seven dollars."

"Yeah. That's a good idea. Give us one a them."

The hombre nodded his shaggy head with nearsighted approval
then ambled off behind the cinder block social center to retrieve the
goods. Pretty soon he rounded the far corner of the building, cradling
a brown paper sack laden with the untaxed booty of a wino's dream.
Seven wrinkled one-dollar bills took roost in his outstretched palm.
The goods changed title, then everyone in the car took their honored
turn at the fiery ritual. John pulled the Pontiac around in the direction
of Chapman Highway and set out for the old rock quarry on Stone
Road.

Sex was in the air. Juicy jugs and loamy loins. "It's Only Make
Believe" by Conway Twitty was playing on the radio as Orbit nervously
eyed a bodacious pair of ta-tas to his port bow about nine o'clock
high. His uncertainty as a cherry-laden freshman caused his hands to
tremble. His whole carcass literally shook and rattled. Then the bottle
of liquid propellant was passed back again from the cockpit, which
he wiped off gallantly with his sleeve. Orbit held up his humble offering to his lady in waiting with a comic bow. Suzie giggled, cocked
her head back to drink, scrutinizing her back seat Casanova full in the
kisser with a long appraising gaze as she quaffed down a full inch of
90 proof love. Then she handed the square-jugged container over to
Prince Charming, laid her head down quietly on his freshly benighted

shoulder, and kissed him softly on the cheek. His heart took wings and flew out the window!

It was easy. But he felt as though he had just won the 26-mile marathon. Thank you, God! he thought in ecstasy. Her hand quickly found its way to his pants zipper, and before you could say beat me, fuck me, make me write bad checks, Mister Littlejohn was standing tall. Never in all his overly protected, post-war existence had he experienced anything so deliciously grand. Pounding his pud didn't hold a candle by comparison. The wild sensations so erotically new to him of Suzie hand-jobbing his tally whacker to blue-steel heaven stole his breath away. With knees braced apart, Orbit slid his hand around her waist, then up beneath her sweater just like he'd read in a sex scene from one of his mother's midnight readers. Suzie wore no undergarments. He would forever remember this night and sweet, sexy Suzie and the rock quarry and Hank Ballard and the Midnighters singing "Annie Had a Baby."

"Oh, baby," she whispered. "Oh, baby."

With a familiar twist of the steering wheel, John wheeled off Stone Road onto the gravel driveway leading back to the rock quarry. Great clouds of rock dust swirled up in starlit balloons following their abrupt passage. Before them lay a magical silver world complimented by a full moon. Red glanced over at the couple in the back seat, licking the sweat off his upper lip, remembering his first time with Carolyn Harris. Flute Weasel was humping her now; nevertheless, he thought about his Cheerleader Princess every day of the week. Paradise Lost.

It was Orbit's big night to shine.

Bubba was half-sloshed, slumped against the passenger door, dreaming about his future.

John was reflecting about his friend Orbit and this special night of baptism, a few yards up ahead, which they all were about to share with Miss Suzie, and the infamous Stone Road rock quarry of South Knoxville, Tennessee.

Chapter Four

Samantha

Somehow, it appeared the young men and women on the dance floor had transmogrified themselves into monstrous genitalia in a stroboscopic dream. Surreal phantoms of erotica, wheeling merrily about in their nebulous gossamer vortex. Ids, egos, and superegos hoisting sail on the morning tide for Xanadu. She, pressing her willing thigh between his randy legs, her hot, voluptuous pelvis a sensual reminder of her sex. He, impassioned wantonly, kissing her full on the lips, his tongue inside her hungry mouth like a greedy, blind red snake. Entwined, circling, nipples impaling hairless chests. The pagan dance of sacrificial rites before the seminiferous deflowering of youth. Their rhythmic caricature of arousal and pain.

There! His hand on her shapely bottom, igneous vaults of bubbling magma just beneath the pubic surface.

And there! Her silken undercarriage wet with anticipation, eager for the night. Both arms wrapped around his neck, suckling a purple hickey on the jugular vein of a Private First Class.

Anatomical fires of the young, driving their elevators up and down until the cables fray and squeal and burn. Awash with one another in time. Forever alone. Shipwrecked together on a lost primordial shore among fierce Jurassic carnivores. Flirting, falling in love, falling out of love, surviving, breaking down the barrier weeds with circles upon circles upon more circles. The bitch in heat, with the glassy-eyed stud hopping about on spavined hind legs, vying with the pack for the mount.

He felt faint, wilted, and cotton-mouthed. Too little sleep and too many pills. And one innocent tab of purple haze. UT exams were finally over. Reaching out her hand she placed a gentle palm against his forehead, just as his mother had done so many times before to check his temperature when he was a child.

Genuine concern reflected back from her mysterious depths. "Are you all right?" she asked.

He knew then that he loved her, so much so that he wanted to cry. "I'm just tired," he said. "Maybe if I had some coffee."

Bubba likewise was concerned. Blotter acid and those west coast turnarounds had knocked John's dick in the dirt. "Sit tight, wild man. I'll get the waitress."

The perfume she wore invaded the corridors of his mind like mustard gas, burning away everything in its path, leaving only the purest residue of passion and desire. The Mound of Venus or the Gallows of Doom! John felt the ice spider web beneath his feet as Samantha turned to face him, smiling, her knee touching his. Her vibrant presence filled his mouth with dirty marbles, stilted phrases, and ugly hop toads. He was the Titanic, plowing desperately through a night fog when the iceberg hove into view. A condemned prisoner, blindfolded before the bulleted wall as the Captain of the Guard marshals the firing squad. Only in dreams had he imagined anyone so utterly feminine and beautiful. Hoping blindly that someday he would meet his dream fantasy, creator of mischief and merriment, the strainer of his greens. And there she sat right beside him. They had just met in Bill's Barn. But the pills and Wild Turkey had rendered him the village idiot.

Coffee arrived. He gulped it down and ordered another one. After his second cup the caffeine kicked in and he felt a little better. Samantha offered to drive him home but he declined, saying he'd best go with Bubba. He didn't want Samantha to see him in a worse light than she had already. Thanking her for her concern and promising to call her the next day, John beat a fading retreat toward the front exit. He almost made it.

Bubba grabbed John's arm as his knees buckled crossing the dance floor. Samantha rushed up quickly on the other side, lending her support. Between the two of them they half walked, half dragged John to the car. There they stashed their 170-pound prize in the back seat. Samantha gave Bubba directions to her place, then climbed in beside "her man." He had managed a good impression in spite of himself. Samantha looked upon John, just as he saw her, as someone she had often dreamt about and longed to meet all her adult life. Her dream fantasy had just fallen asleep.

Chapter Five

Romance

Weeks passed as the two lovers became more and more enamored of one another. It was the first time in his life John had known the true love of a woman. Samantha was mad about John and his devotion to her. Even his parents approved, which was a real first. Sam's mother, Miss Martha, told Samantha she thought John was a great catch.

Samantha worked for the Alcoa Aluminum Company of America. She had a small house in Alcoa, provided her by the company officials. During the week she lived there, often taking her work home with her at night. Most weekends she returned to South Knoxville to spend time with her mother in Colonial Village. With John in the picture, Sam was spending most of her free time with John, who in turn was spending most of his free time with Samantha. Miss Martha didn't mind a bit. She wanted what was best for her little girl.

Part of Samantha's job description was showing dignitaries around Metro Knoxville whenever they visited the smelting plant in Alcoa.

Places like Gatlinburg and The University of Tennessee were of special interest. She showed them the local reservoirs of the Tennessee Valley Authority, the Fort Loudon Dam in Lenoir City, and maps and charts of the TVA flood control system which ran 400 miles west to the Mississippi River. She drove them to see where Civil War battles had been fought, explained the regional growth patterns moving north and west, Knoxville's proximity to Nashville and Chattanooga, and the area's excellent school systems. She introduced them to the Chamber of Commerce and the Tennessee Theatre. Knoxville was a major expressway hub 200 miles north of Atlanta, so there was ample potential for growth and prosperity.

The Paris Café was a new restaurant in West Knoxville. Sam took John there on their second date. John loved the place. The food was excellent, but most of all John enjoyed the African piano player who joked and laughed with his audience and sang like nothing John had ever heard before. This became their favorite night spot in Knoxville. Sam introduced John to Angelina Jones, the owner and one of Knoxville's movers and shakers. A friendship was struck. Over the next few months they visited The Paris Café on average of once a week.

Eva and Little Ike provided the singing and musical entertainment at the Brown Derby out west on Kingston Pike, but the dance place they liked best was the Carnival Club north of town on Clinton Highway. Another adventurous scene was Cumberland Avenue which ran through the UT area downtown, which everyone called The Strip. School kids and young adults flocked there to dance and party. The University of Tennessee was a party school. More than a few students flunked out because they allowed themselves to get caught up in all the fun and excitement.

Samantha noticed that John seldom studied. She asked about this several times, but vague replies were all she ever received from John. She noted, too, that he drank too much. On several occasions she drove them home rather than allow John behind the steering wheel. This began to trouble Samantha. She worried that he might get pulled over for driving under the influence, or worse yet flunk out of school. Minor arguments ensued. Sam was a hard worker and she expected the same thing from John. She never had the opportunity to go to college, and it troubled her that John wasn't buckling down and taking life more seriously. Education was a wonderful thing, something that couldn't be taken away from an individual. Time was the enemy of higher education. Either a person applied themselves and made the grade, or they were left standing on the side of life with those less fortunate. Sam began to fret, wondering if maybe she had made a mistake.

Chapter Six

Carnival Club

John came to, naked and viciously hungover, with vomit caked to his face and in his hair. It was clotted in the leaves where he lay in the front yard shrubbery of a red brick residence he had never seen before. It's cold, he thought drowsily, not fully realizing if he was awake or dreaming. A sickly sweet stench caused him to convulse violently, his eyes bulging with pain, two labored spasms tasting of iron bile and mucus. The inside of his head resembled a three-alarm fire. He remembered nothing of how he got there or how he came to be naked, covered with puke. Panic came slithering through the grass but he didn't understand why. He only knew he was in serious trouble unless he pulled his act together and got out of there pronto. Then he remembered…moldy bits and pieces of his insecure jealousy and rage.

They had been at the Carnival Club where Sam was high and having a great time. She danced with some of the men who asked her, but he couldn't handle it and swelled up like a blowfish. He was shit-faced, which usually made him ten times more the jealous yahoo when he felt his manhood was being flogged with another man's dick. He didn't understand what made him paranoid when he drank. But he had read about people with all sorts of head ailments in his psychology classes. It had to do with not coping well or being a dick-head or some such hypothetical Freudian song and dance. John had yet to comprehend that alcohol was a depressant. So there he was, lost, with no fucking clothes, in some stranger's yard, underneath a million stars out in the fucking cold. Then he remembered slamming the car keys down on the table and storming out of the club, yelling at Sam that she was a whore. Jesus! So he had to be off Clinton Highway someplace. Yeah. He had come out the back door, cut across an open field…his clothes were in that field.

Car lights flashed across his prone position as an automobile passed through the darkness on its way to an unknown rendezvous. He shivered with the cold, marveling at the jeweled beauty of a black velvet sky. His nocturnal kingdom. John loved the night. His silent sanctuary. He had loved it ever since he was a little boy when his daddy and Bob Sams took him possum hunting. His dad took the possums they treed and killed to the black gang working at his father's tire store back in Knoxville.

Sometimes the nights were pitch black, but most times the stars were out and there was a piece of a moon lighting the way. Full moons were best. The fields and trees shone like quicksilver, and there was a bright reverence upon the land. He remembered the sounds of the dogs and the laughter of his father and Mister Sams. He missed the shooting stars, the pungent odor of skunk riding the crisp night air, the kinship one felt with nature, and especially the tiny glowworms. They gave off little patches of light all across the fields. And always off in the distance somewhere was the mournful cry of a locomotive, calling him to arms and faraway adventure. But something had gone wrong. He had become older and jaded. Now he had little time for his devoted mother and father.

His panic returned with the vision of Sam's hurt and angry face when he accused her of flaunting herself at the characters in the roadhouse. Down deep he knew she wasn't anything like that, but the alcohol and the sight of her having such a good time dancing with other men had activated something hateful and selfish inside him. Everyone danced with everyone else at that nightclub.

The thought of losing Sam terrified him, so he lashed out drunkenly, saying she acted like a whore, accusing her of just using him for sex. She cried then, but he couldn't let it go. She didn't love him at all, he railed. She was a goddamned gold digger after his daddy's money. The bouncer came over then, asking them to leave. He smashed his fist into the young man's face, sending him crashing through a table behind theirs. Madness welled up in his head and he hit the bouncer again, then he flung down the car keys on the table and bolted across the room and out the back door.

Then he ran. He ran like a thing damned of all deliverance from the monsters of his subconscious mind…fear of himself. Fear he wasn't good enough. Fear of social rejection and ridicule. Fear especially of not being good enough for Samantha. Fear of not being smart enough in school. Fear of having to face a strange world he didn't understand, which frightened him to no end. Fear of his ultimate discovery, humiliation, and final defeat.

He ran until he stumbled and fell headlong in a plowed field half a mile behind the Carnival Club. He rolled there in the dirt like a stricken animal, pain and humiliation streaming out every pore. His childish jealousy over Sam, coupled with an overdose of rotgut whiskey, had catapulted him into a dark, ambivalent state of mind. He wept brokenly, with his back pressed to a wheeling earth, then vomited all over himself.

Drunk as he was, he reasoned that he must purge himself of his shortcomings. Since he fancied himself a defrocked outcast and an unappreciated piece of dog shit, his soiled clothing appeared credible.

Off they came, shoes, pants, socks, the works, where he abandoned them in the moonlit field. The misery and confusion storming inside his whiskey-soaked brain drove him on another 100 yards where he hunkered down, exhausted, and passed out.

John struggled up from Mother Nature's bed and breakfast, raked off his gelatinous face and hair with his fingers, crouched down low, nearly pitching forward into the shrubbery, then trotted back out the way he had come in, with his shriveled dong slapping back and forth between his thighs. Jesus God! he thought miserably. If I get outta this one it'll be a miracle. How can I be so friggin' stupid? The rocks and briars hurt his tender feet and legs, and just then he stumbled into a barbed wire fence. "Son of a Bitch!" he exploded. His stomach was cut and bleeding but no real damage was done. On through the pebbles and pine cones he hippity-hopped, wincing with every painful step. There in the moonlight he saw the field. The moon's illumination carried him back again to fishing trips and possum hunting and those bygone years of a happy childhood.

Stepping out onto the plowed earth, he felt a sense of relief. Its cool, moist texture was soothing to his bruised and aching feet. Even his head felt better from the night air. About twenty yards up ahead and off to the right he saw a silver shoe in the moonlight. That's it, he thought. I'll take my clothes down to that creek beside the highway, wash myself up, then make tracks for home. Sam's got her car so I'll call her in the morning and apologize. Maybe she won't be too pissed off at me for acting like a crazy asshole. The fear swept over him again in such a painful tide that he lowered his weary frame down on the ground and prayed to God Almighty for Samantha's forgiveness.

Down on the deck, spraddle-kneed, huddled over himself in pious grace, his ass resting in the dirt, he thought how gentle and sweet she had been with him ever since they began dating last spring. She was a kind and wonderful lady. And such a treat in bed!

"God, please Jesus, let her take me back," he prayed. "I love her. I need this woman. Please, God, I'm no good without Sammy. Let her forgive me. I love Samantha," he whispered.

In his mind's eye he saw Samantha holding on to the headboard of her queen-size bed the last time they made love. They were doing it doggie-style. His erection grew to its full length where he sat in the silver earth, all by his naked lonesome, in a farmer's plowed field sixteen miles from home. He closed his eyes to concentrate on her beautiful behind, thrusting back at him until she was panting for breath. He gave it to her full-bore, causing her to cry out with pleasure. His hand slid up and down his shaft more rapidly now. Samantha was approaching her climax. Small beads of perspiration were gathered across her brow as she gazed back at him with sex-glazed eyes.

"Oh, Johnny!" she gasped. "I love you, honey!"

Then she trembled violently as the orgasmic fires in her belly rushed forth. One final pump of his hand and a liquid salvo of fire ejaculated into the surrounding universe.

"Please, God. Let her forgive me," he begged. And pitched forward face down in the rich, moist earth.

Chapter Seven

Morning

Samantha opened her eyes, her makeup still on. Light was streaming between the curtains of the bedroom window, creating a prism of sunshine across the bottom of her bed and halfway up the opposite wall. Dust particles appeared suspended in the limpid beam as if they were tiny planets drifting in a golden void of cosmic miniatures. Her dress and stockings lay in a crumpled pile on the floor beside the bed. She still wore her bra and panties. Then she remembered the night before, and driving herself home.

Shame flooded her senses. Anger. Betrayal. Alarm. Had any of her friends been inside the club when John threw his temper tantrum? God, what a scene! What would people think? He was such a spoiled brat, playing his macho games and running around with those wild friends of his. Yet she loved him so much, she began to cry. Quiet, muffled sobs with tears streaming out both corners of her blonde lashes.

"Damn you!" she whispered. "Oh, damn you, John!"

She sat up in bed, eyes wide open, remembering having danced with three different men. Maybe she shouldn't have, but where was the harm? The other girls danced with the regulars. It was just accepted. She had never seen their dates make a fuss, much less start a fight. John had ruined everything with his childish jealousy. And called her a whore. And a gold digger! Who the hell did he think he was? The ungrateful wretch! All those nights together and she never looked at another man. Nor even thought about one.

Maybe it was true what they said about men's brains being down there in their pants. He was so insistent sometimes it was almost a turnoff. Why did they have to do it every time he came over? Why, just once, couldn't they hold hands and just enjoy one another's company? John was a spoiled pain in the ass, she thought. If she allowed him to get away with stunts like this he'd never grow up. He wasn't ready for marriage or even holding down a steady job. Lord knows she loved him, though. But no way was this right. No damn way! She had to put her foot down right now or their relationship was headed for the rocks. She wouldn't tolerate his brutish behavior one more day.

She showered and dressed and set about the task of preparing her breakfast. Her head hurt. Then the telephone rang. Samantha considered not answering the noisy thing but decided if it was John this was the right time to confront the issue.

"But Sam, I was drunk. I'm sorry. I was just drunk, that's all. I didn't mean the things I said."

"You were out of control, John. You acted like you were on drugs or something."

"I know. It was the booze. It makes me crazy sometimes."

"Then why do you drink so much?"

"Sam, I don't know. I'm sorry, OK?"

"No! It's not OK. You're not OK."

"Well, you danced with those guys. What was I supposed to do?"

"Try acting like a gentleman once in a while instead of all the drinking and being the life of the party. You're smart. You have brains. But you're blowing it. In school, with your parents, you don't even know how to treat me."

"But I love you. That's something, isn't it?"

"Damn it, you aren't listening to me. Grow up! Accept responsibility. Do you think your father is proud of the way you fool around in school? Do you think I am?"

"What I do in school is my business. My old man likes me well enough."

"Your father loves you, John. But you're too stuck on yourself to know how much he worries about you. It's the same way with your mother, and me too."

"What do you mean, 'me too'?"

"Last night you threw a fit because I danced with some strangers. The others do it all the time. It was harmless fun. But did we discuss it like mature adults? Noooo. You had to start a big fight and make fools of us both right in front of everybody. And that poor man you hit had to have stitches."

"That's his problem. He shouldn't have grabbed my arm."

"That's right! Blame it on somebody else. Mister Perfect has the right to go around getting drunk and beating people up."

"I didn't mean to hurt him. Let's stop all this arguing. I'll come over tonight and…"

"No! I don't want to see you again until you learn to behave. I'll not have you embarrassing me by acting like a drunken idiot. Grow up, John. Stop running away."

"That's not fair. I care about you."

"Then prove it."

"How?"

"Stop hiding in a liquor bottle. Make something of yourself in school."

"I'm working on it. Let me see you tonight."

"No, John. I'm serious. Stay away from me until you've gotten your head on straight. When I'm ready to see you again, I'll call you. Now, good-bye."

Before he could answer she hung up on him. She didn't know she was going to hang up, she just did it. Damn him! She felt shaky and sick to her stomach. Samantha stared down sadly at her cold plate of scrambled eggs and buttered toast. So much for breakfast, she thought. So much for leisure Sunday drives in the country. So much for dreams of having a family. She wondered if John really had what it takes to make a go of things. Too many of her girlfriends had husbands and boyfriends like that. She wondered how they managed to be a wife and a guidance counselor all at the same time. The phone rang again so she took it off the hook and walked back to her bedroom. Happy memories flooded her thoughts, then the sad ones poured in. They had never had a serious fight before. Samantha lay down on the bed, curled up in the fetal position, and wept until she fell into a fitful sleep. Then she dreamed.

She felt the wet sponges against her skin beneath the tight leather straps securing her arms and legs to the heavy apparatus. The big wooden chair felt strangely comfortable. Waves of fear filled her throat with the sour taste of stomach bile, making it difficult to swallow. She was gagged with the sash of her wedding gown, securing a balled-up marriage license stuffed in her mouth. The tart smell of ammonia permeated her nostrils with the odor of her own sweat. Across the room, seemingly far away in a deranged nightmare, sat twelve jurors, tried and true. They were seated together, awaiting the light show. John was front row center. He was yelling at her and cursing. The others were the men she had dated a time or two, or gone to bed with before she met John.

John got up and walked away. She couldn't see him anymore but the lighting cast his shadow with spectral effects on a vertical wall beyond the voyeurs of the jury. He was around the corner of the L-shaped room, poised beside a raised steel switch with a long rubber handle. She wanted to complain about the dreadful shadow but the license in her mouth prevented her from doing so. What difference would it make, anyway? She waited patiently while Father Barthalamaeus made her peace with God, then shifted her attention back to the awful lure of the wall. In surreal horror, the dark arm of the shadow moved out in slow motion, taking hold of the rubber handle, then jerked down violently. Twenty-two hundred volts of executional fire exploded through her brain on their maiden voyage to everywhere. She felt the electricity arcing between her teeth. Stars faded to black as her convulsed body continued to hammer against the cruel leather bindings.

She awoke with a start, the nightmare vivid and real. Her first impulse was to call John and ask him to come over. Talk things out. She missed him already. But, just as quickly, she realized that would be a fatal mistake. She didn't want to lose him, but neither did she want him carrying on like a drunken fool. He had to put his nose to the grindstone and get on with the process of becoming a man. Or John Henry Jackson would never amount to a hill of beans.

"I'm in love with a lunatic." she said out loud. "He's driving me crazy. "

She had never had such a savage, disturbing dream before. The baneful aberration of John pulling the switch hung like a shroud in her pained resentment. Did it mean John was killing their relation-ship? Had she become the victim? Had John become his own victim? Samantha hoped none of it was true. She just wanted him whole and happy and back in her arms again.

Chapter Eight

The Yard Arm

John was stone miserable without Samantha. Lost. Vulnerable. Fucked up. The fire in him had blown out as if it never existed. He felt sorry for himself. Maimed. Rejected. Rode hard and put up wet. He couldn't eat nor sleep. The world was not an attractive place without the strainer of his greens by his side, paying proper attention to his manly needs. No, it had all turned to guano. Shit! Bubba called earlier that morning but John put him off, saying his stomach was out of sorts. He had never treated Bubba that way before. He was drinking more too. Much more. Floundering around in a bourbon sea of unresolved self-pity.

Tonight he was slumped forward, elbows on the countertop, astride a barstool at the Yard Arm on Forest Avenue. An avant-garde, Lysol-scrubbed liquor parlor managed by his intellectual friend Roger Carroll. The place catered to poor area residents and even poorer university students with bare-bones allowances afforded them lovingly by their struggling mamas and poppas. Painted concrete floors and old fishnets with cork floats decorated the ancient interior. Toward the east, out beyond Mascot and Strawberry Plains, John heard the inbound whistle of an L&N freight hauling coal to the TVA steam plant in Kingston. The lonesome sound pricked an exposed nerve in the psychic stuffing of his miserable interior, causing the hair on his neck and arms to rise up.

He tossed off the last of his buck twenty-five bourbon and Coke and ordered another round. Four drinks in front of that one, plus little sleep in three nights had given him a solid buzz. He mused about his sad predicament. What the hell am I going to do? he asked himself for the hundredth time that day.

The thought of being run over by a freight train had a certain romantic appeal. The whistle drifted through the open door a second time. She'd be sorry then, by God. The Knoxville News Sentinel headlines would lament his passing.

"Rejected South Knoxville Youth Crushed Beneath Cruel Wheels of Love." "The University of Tennessee to Honor John Henry Jackson With Rededication of Ayres Hall."

"Ole Stonewall would be proud," he said to himself.

"Samantha Fox Jumped Today From the Henley Street Bridge to Join Her Dead Sweetheart. Body Remains Found in Murky Waters of Fort Loudon Lake. He Loved Her Wet or Dry. Families Mourn."

He gave himself over freely to his boozy flirtation. Daydreaming was a favorite pastime with John. Off in the distance he could hear it coming, full throttle. Casey Jones hauls down on the whistle but this is a nightmare, only John is awake and can't move. Slowly the noise factor builds. In his Ancient Age surroundings the earth begins to tremble and shake. Again and again the frantic warning sounds, but John's sorry ass is in limbo. Feets don't fail me now, but that phone call to Sam had snapped his spine like a dry twig. In mind-fuck paralysis he emptied his glass a sixth time, watching helplessly as the great squalling beast bore down mightily on his petrified soul. The engineer was Samantha, blonde hair flying in the wind, sparks and smoke boiling from the smokestack, returning a few personal baubles plus an armload of records he'd collected over the years. One final blast from the screaming whistle and the cowcatcher slammed him a double loop, straight into the briar patch.

"That fucking bitch!" he blurted out.

"Whaddayasay?"

The angular stranger seated at the end of the bar was feeling no pain himself. Bill Paul was a Marine veteran, circa helicopter pilot, on the GI Bill at UT majoring in beer and pussy. Bell-bottom jeans and a white turtleneck sweater complimented his shoulder-length brown hair and full mustache. A silver peace medallion hung down on his broad chest from a string of spent grenade pins around his neck. The Yard Arm was his nocturnal retreat, his Playboy mansion away from Math and English. Here he scored with the willing coeds, taking them back to his three-room flat across Forest Avenue for free lessons in the horizontal shuffle. The girls thought him quaint, even heroic, oooohing and aaaahing over the devil dog tattooed on his muscular shoulder. He was such a man!

"She run me down!"

"No shit. Whadda she do it for?"

"Cause I'm a asshole."

"No shit. Pleasetameetcha. I'm a asshole my damn self."

John smiled for the first time that day. A big barnyard grin.

"Let's drink to it, my asshole to your asshole. Mano a mano."

The smiling veteran saw in John a kindred drinking companion. Someone to help him forget the things he'd seen and done in Vietnam, his personal Heart of Darkness. John's next drink went down so easy he ordered a double for himself and another Schlitz for his friend, William.

"You ever been in love, Mister Bill?"

"Yeah, one time."

"What happened to 'er?"

"Her father sent her away to school to break it up."

"What a shitty... How could he do something like that?"

Baptist minister. You know…pillar of society. The usual twisted shit."

"You ever see 'er again?"

"No, I joined the Corps after she left."

"No shit. You still love 'er?"

"No. Think about her sometimes, though. Two tours in Vietnam changed a lot of things. I guess she's married by now."

"Was it bad in Vietnam? You ever kill anybody?"

"It was bad sometimes. Most of the time it was just boring as hell. You know, the usual official bullshit. Yes, sir…no, sir…hurry up and wait."

"Some news dork said the other day that the war oughta be over by Christmas. You think it'll be?"

"Not likely."

"How come?"

"Cause Johnson and Westmoreland don't understand what they're up against."

"No shit! I always heard Johnson was sorta crooked. They said he rigged his first election down in Texas. When you think we'll win?"

"Maybe we won't win. Maybe we'll just bleed like the frogs. Got their ass kicked boo koo big time at Dien Bien Phu."

"What's a frog?"

"It's slang for French. They eat frog legs, snails, caviar, things like that."

"All right! But how could we lose?"

"The French were there a hundred years and Ho Chi Minh drove them out."

"I'll be damned."

"The French were bastards. Treated the Vietnamese people like nigger stepkids. Hell, Vichy France joined the Nazis during the Second World War."

"That's fucking unreal. How come you know so much?"

"I read the history of Vietnam while I was over there. Them people been fightin' for 2,000 years. Little dudes tough as nails."

"But they're communists. They're our enemies."

"They're communists all right, some of them anyways. But Ho Chi Minh was our friend during World War Two. His men used to rescue American flyers shot down by the Japanese. Probably woulda got their independence from France if FDR hadn't kicked the bucket. I think Truman screwed 'em over for NATO."

"No shit! Then why we tryin' to kill his ass?"

"Hell if I know? The clowns in Washington screwed up in the final days of the Second World War by not recognizing Ho Chi Minh as a potential Asian Tito. Our Secret Service was over there fighting the Japanese. Major Patti knew Ho Chi Minh. He told Washington the dude seemed all right. But all the bureaucrats could see were the words 'communist sympathizer.' So Uncle Ho's requests for official recognition by Uncle Sam for a free Vietnam went down the crapper."

"Sounds like my fucked-up love life."

"You can fix your love life. Thing is, if we cut and pull out now, the whole damn region could go to hell in a commie-ass handbag."

The new friends continued to drink until they were both roaring drunk. Roger finally suggested they "refrain from the grape before they wash out to sea." So Bill herded John across the street to his three-room hacienda and made him a place to sleep on the couch. In the days to follow, Bill Paul would have a maturing effect on both John and Bubba.

Chapter Nine

Mom and Dad

Frank and Mildred Jackson were in a pickle. They didn't know what to do with John. Bubba had visited their home the night before to talk with them about John's drinking and his personal concerns over John and Samantha. Everyone knew about the breakup. Sam had called two days earlier to discuss the situation and to ask for any advice they had to offer. Mister and Missus Jackson were quite fond of Samantha Fox. They believed she would make a fine wife for their bouncing baby boy. But John was falling through the cracks and nobody seemed to have a clue how to straighten him out.

Frank went to work that morning feeling the stress of a concerned parent. His independent tire business was on the decline due to all the corporate competition coming out of Chicago and Detroit, so he was thinking about selling out. His General Tire dealership had been good to him and his family for 27 years. Selling General Tires had made him a successful and respected businessman in the community. Mister

Jackson had his eye on a tract of lakefront property across the river, in Blount County, which he believed would make a good subdivision. The land was reasonable at $1,000 an acre and he wanted a change of scenery. The house was paid for, they had money in the bank, and Mildred was in favor of it. But his son was another matter. They had to come up with something before John found himself in a real jam.

For the better part of a week John had been holed up at Bill Paul's apartment next door to the university campus and Ayres Hall. Bubba finally located the two, after hitting all the bars on The Strip, drinking together at the Yard Arm. That a.m. after John was nicely tucked in on-board his sofa, three sheets to the wind, Bubba and the veteran talked.

"He ain't thinkin' real straight. He feels sorry for his ass and all that happy crap, but he's a good feller. Trouble is, he ain't never had to prove nothin'."

"Well, hell. Me neither," answered Bubba.

"You're different, man. Kinda country, like me. John is all city inside, like a girl. But in a good way. He takes things to heart, like, too much. I guess you know about that girl of his?"

"Yeah, Sam's cool…bent out of shape, though. His mom and dad are too."

"I reckon they are. You two ever think about the military?"

"Yeah, I think about it sometimes. Both my uncles were in the Army."

"It's a good place to sort things out. Me and John talked about it some. He don't like school much, does he?"

"He got a C average. Nothin' to write home about."

"What kinda grades you got?"

"C plus."

"Both a you oughta be up there in them As an' Bs."

"I oughta be a lotta things, but I can't seem to get it off the ground."

"It takes discipline. You gotta want it."

"I wish I could be like my father. He's got discipline out the ass."

"You can be any damn thing you want to be." The veteran looked Bubba square in the face. "Join the Marines for two years. Come back and finish school. Get married and raise a family."

"What about the war? What if I get sent over there?"

"No big deal, man. Odds are you'll make it back OK. Keep your eyes open and mind your own business. It's one hell of a by-god experience."

Bubba didn't sleep well that night thinking about all the things he and Bill Paul had discussed. Join the Marines. Finish school. Get married. Dang! The more he tossed and turned, with daylight peeking through the window shades, the better it began to sound. A college degree and a wife! Far out, man.

That noon Bubba met John for lunch at the Ellis & Ernest Drug Store on the UT campus.

"Here's the deal. We got nothin' goin' for us around here. Why not join the Marines for two years and see the world? That would make Sam and your parents real proud. The Marines, man. Think about it."

"You and Bill are some kinda gung ho idiots. What about Vietnam?"

"Fuck Vietnam! If we're lucky we won't have to go. But if we do, we'll make it back OK."

"How the hell do you know that? Guys are getting killed over there every day."

"You see us getting killed? We're the original Brothers Grimm. Semper Fi and a big Moon Pie."

"Shit fire! Brother Bill has really been indoctrinating your crazy ass!"

"Yes, he has. He's somebody special. He told me things I never saw before."

"Like what?"

"Gettin' my shit together. Comin' back and finishing school.

Finding myself a girl and settling down. I'm tired of all this partying bullshit."

"You're serious, aren't you?"

"Serious as a heart attack. We'll get drafted anyway. So why not choose what we want? You gonna piss around and lose Sam at the rate you're goin'."

That one stopped John dead in his tracks. In his own self-centered way he loved Sam more than he favored himself. Maybe Bubba had a plan. The draft was hanging over their heads. Two years wasn't forever. But would she understand? Would she be there when he returned home? Right then he decided to ask Sam to marry him before he joined the Marine Corps. Would she consent? he wondered. What would his parents think? Could he make the grade as a Marine? John was taking hold for the first time in his life. He noticed something different he had never felt before. It felt right.

Eight o'clock that night Bubba met with Red and Orbit at the Southern Circle. He explained what he and John had decided to do, asking if they wanted to sign up and go with them. Orbit declined, with good reason. He had a scholarship and was on the dean's list at UT. Red had nothing to fall back on and readily agreed. The barefoot boys from Tennessee had just rolled the dice.

Chapter Ten

Wedding Bells

Frank and Mildred cried. Miss Martha and Samantha cried. Mister and Missus Smith cried. Bubba and John cried too, but tried to hide it. It was a beautiful wedding held in the Jackson home with neighbors and friends and all the relatives in attendance. Bill Paul arrived wearing his Marine Corps dress blue uniform. Red and Mister Jackson both noticed the decorations on his chest. Frank never asked, but he knew he was in the presence of a man who had seen things maybe he didn't want to know about.

Nevertheless, he and Mildred had given their blessing to both boys regarding their desire to join the Marines. Bubba's parents were rightly concerned over the welfare of their only son, but they, too, gave their blessing to both boys as well. Draft was in the air, so everyone believed it was the patriotic thing to do. Lieutenant Paul was quite proud of his newly anointed heroes. And Samantha Fox believed her prayers had been answered. It was a new beginning for four young Americans, including Red, in a world of uncertainty and confusion. Israel was preparing for war, Leonid Brezhnev was rattling his Cold War rockets, and China was in the throes of a political upheaval. Meanwhile, the war in Southeast Asia rolled on with only blood and misery at the end of a very dark tunnel.

The reception following the wedding went off without a hitch. And to prove to Samantha that he meant to do the right thing by her, John drank only three toasts of champagne. Nervous? Very. Apprehensive? Yes. Happy? More than either one of them believed possible. Sam glowed and John beamed. When it came time to leave, the "old married couple" ran down the back steps, jumped into John's Pontiac convertible, and drove away on their honeymoon with an assortment of tin cans rattling along behind.

On the outskirts of Knoxville, John pulled over and cut the cans free. Then they proceeded on to Atlanta, Georgia. Sam had been born in Atlanta, where her mother had abandoned her when she was just an infant on the front porch of Martha Fox's home in Dunwoody. Martha took the child in and raised her like her own daughter. Martha never told anyone. For years people assumed Martha had Sam out of wedlock. When Sam was sixteen Martha told Samantha how she came to be her little girl. Sam adored Miss Martha. So, before John left for Parris Island, Sam wanted to see Atlanta one last time and pretend that maybe, just maybe, her mother had finally found her happiness, just as she had found happiness with John Henry Jackson. Samantha Jane Fox Jackson had indeed found her place in the sun.

Atlanta was cool beans in 1967. The Me Generation were smoking begonia weed up and down Peachtree Road, and everyplace else one might purchase a nickel bag. The pill had unburdened women from the age-old bugaboo of getting pregnant, and good girls were giving the stuff away like it was going out of style. There was a carnival atmosphere in the ozone. Folks born in Atlanta were accommodating to all the newcomers moving to town from all over the country, and Ivan

Allen, Jr., was the presiding mayor over an expanding metropolis of nearly half a million people. It was the Age of Aquarius, and Priscilla Ann Beaulieu had just tied the knot with Elvis Presley.

Jim Morrison was the guru of the hippie movement. Janis Joplin lived and sang "Full Tilt Boogie." And Jimi Hendrix would play his "Star-Spangled Banner" before the crowd at Woodstock in 1969. Steppenwolf told of the American drug culture in "Desperation" and "The Pusher," Iron Butterfly was "In-A-Gadda-Da-Vida," and the wiley Mick Jagger up and stole the King's thorny crown. People adored the Bee Gees and went gonzo over Led Zepplin. The Beatles were a household name, and Bob Dylan became the voice of American protest.

John Portman's downtown Hyatt Regency was an architectural triumph straight out of a science fiction novel. Twenty-two stories of glass, steel girders, and reinforced concrete with an enormous atrium inside the hollow structure, and glass elevators reminiscent of Buck Rogers and Flash Gordon. There was a revolving blue Plexiglass restaurant on top of the building, offering diners a 360-degree panoramic view of the neighboring countryside. During a brisk wind, one could watch the hanging decorations inside the restaurant move to and fro because the building had been designed to sway several inches during a storm.

Samantha and John were lodged on the top floor, facing north toward Buckhead and Sandy Springs. Down below sparkled the New Tara of a New South. A regal setting which one hundred years before lay in chaos and ruin. It wasn't until 1939, when Gone With the Wind played to a packed house at the Loews Grand Theatre on Peachtree Road, that the South finally regained her stolen dignity. Yankee carpetbaggers had taken everything that wasn't nailed down after General Sherman burned part of the city to the ground in 1864. Scarlett O'Hara and Rhett Butler had remained all too familiar for boys and girls growing up in the Old South.

John's own pride and maturity were evolving by leaps and bounds beside his beautiful Samantha. A man-seed had been planted and was growing in the fertile soil of his Southern heritage. Samantha Fox was a natural-born Southern belle. The two of them together made a striking couple. They made love for hours, sharing with one another their hopes and dreams for their future together. It was a time of discovery and great happiness between John and Samantha.

They visited the High Museum of Art, the Governor's Mansion, Joe Tierney's famous restaurant on Roswell Road, Mickey Lawson's art gallery, the Fox Theatre, Harrison's on Peachtree, and the Atlanta Zoo with Willie B. the Gorilla. They enjoyed an assortment of landmarks and restaurants. And Samantha finally found the closure she sought. Her birth mother was an illusion. She had never been there for Sam. Miss Martha was her mama now. Samantha was living the all-American dream. She had a happy marriage and a bright future. Her whole world had turned around in the brief span of four weeks. It was time to go home.

Driving back to Knoxville proved just as enjoyable as the trip to Atlanta. They had discovered one another in that magical and special way with soul mates. A spiritual bond had been forged. Samantha loved and trusted John. No longer did she fear that her love for him was a mistake. In his role as husband, John was emerging as her white knight in a sky blue Pontiac convertible. Now it was time to pay his dues as a United States Marine.

Chapter Eleven

Semper Fidelis (always faithful)

Parris Island

"Get off the bus! Get off the bus! Out! Out! Out! Out!"

John and Bubba looked at one another in surprised shock. The other recruits stood up with dazed looks on their faces, then began shuffling single file toward the front door as fast as their narrow quarters would allow. Red, John, and Bubba followed suit. Organized pandemonium. A Drill Instructor was right behind them howling, "Get out! Get out!"

Through the windows of the Greyhound bus they could see a second Drill Instructor pacing back and forth beside the bus, swinging a swagger stick up and down into his open palm, screaming instructions at the confused and intimidated "Marines."

They were supposed to be confused and intimidated. This was the beginning of a thirteen-week siege of specialized shock treatment designed by experts. Intensive boot camp training by tush-hog mother-fuckers and ferocious sons-a-bitches. The Waffen SS and the KGB served up on the half shell.

The objective was simple. Break down the civilian recruits into their original subhuman species known throughout the Island as "maggots." Take away their sluglike identities. Scrap their previous bullshit existence. Deprive them of pogey bait (candy), fags (cigarettes), mama san (mother), and Coca-Cola. Shave their stupid heads. Kick their worthless asses. Scream in their filthy ears. And drill each sorry platoon until they farted smoke rings and pissed steam. Instill upon one and all that they were nothing before the United States Marine Corps. Useless sacks of shit! A blight on God, Old Glory, and John Wayne. But now they're in the Corps and they're still useless sacks of shit! Maggots! Shit birds! Pussies! But, with the aid of your noble Drill Instructors, each and every one a blood brother to Chesty Puller, and a sworn disciple to the Cause of Freedom and Death Before Dishonor, you might…it's fucking unlikely…but you might actually graduate some sunny day from beautiful, exotic Parris Island and become a United States Marine!

The twenty-one newcomers were screamed at and chased across the parade grounds. The draftees running full tilt with their personal belongings flapping in the breeze, the volunteers bobbing along in their muddled wake, gasping for breath with their heavy duffle bags in tow. Their assigned staging area was in front of a two-story wooden barracks where more confused citizens stood at attention in the start of a new platoon. This thoroughly rattled menagerie was on hold, awaiting the final busload which would bring their numerical strength up to the required platoon number of seventy-five USMC recruits.

Finally, the last dozen arrived. "You fucking people fall in…on the double! Get it straight, ya herd a yo-yos. Arms right! Form it up like ya had some sense. One arm's length apart."

It was considered essential that they learn to stand perfectly still at attention. Movement of any kind for whatever reason was not tolerated. Later, in the jungles of Vietnam, they would understand why. Their DI spotted one of the recruits rubbernecking.

"Jesus H. Christ! What's your mother call you, boy?"

"Duh… Duh… Driggins, sir."

"Duh Duh Driggins? Gaddamn! I never heard no such a name. What you looking at, Driggins? You got tha hots for your shit-bird neighbor? Are you one a them mandrakes we been hearin' about? Do you suck cock, Driggins?"

"No, sir."

"Where you from, boy?"

"I'm…uh…North Carolina, sir."

"Sir, I'm from North Carolina, Sir! Do you brainless fucking wonders understand English? I can't hear you!"

"Yes, sir!" Seventy-five recruits answered in unison.

"Sir, yes, Sir! I can't heaaar yooou."

"Sir, yes, Sir!" Much louder now.

"I can't hear you fucking pussies."

"SIR, YES, SIR!" Their strained decibels might have knocked the balls off a brass monkey had one been available.

"You piss me off, Driggins. You know what that means?"

"Sir, no, sir…sir?"

"Sir, no, Sir, maggot! It means I got my eyeballs on you, boy. I'm gonna be watchin' you like a mongoose lookin' at a free meal. Any more you pogey bait fist-fuckers want to socialize? All ya's look like ya'd lean on one ta me! Shit, Miss Agnus! Ain't but one thing worse'n a ankle-grabbin' faggot an' that's a commie rat bastard! Keep yer head and eyes to tha front!

"You there! Who tha fuck gave you permission ta move? Them sand fleas gotta eat too, boy. Fall out and give me twenty push-ups. On the double, mister!

"You fucking people listen up! My name is Dipano. Sergeant Dipano. You will address me as 'Sir, Sergeant Dipano, Sir.' I been assigned to nursemaid you buncha freaks for the privilege and honor uh training you ta serve in the Frenchifried jungles of Vietnam. So, for the next three months, you are mine to keep. Forget about home. Forget about the outside world. Forget ever' thing you ever knew before you came here. You belong to me!

"This here is Sergeant Kohn. In case you're all blind an ignorant, Sergeant Kohn is a Cherokee Indian. Andy Jackson stole his home so he provokes real goddamn easy. Sergeant Kohn is a Korean War veteran and a decorated hero of Vietnam!

"And this stone killer is Sergeant Bear. Any you longhairs got any queer notions about jumpin' tha fence, Sergeant Bear hates fuckin' deserters. Parris Island is the center of the Free World surrounded by tidal swamps and quicksand, cottonmouths and alligators. One way in and one way out. That road is patrolled night and day by summa Sergeant Bear's close friends. Can't do nothin' else. They killed so many Vietcong rat bastards we can't turn 'em loose on society, so we keep 'em here! You go over tha fence you'll get ta meet them in person. The rest a you clowns keep yer noses clean, pay attention in class, don't fuck up, and maybe you'll learn enough to stay tha fuck alive! At ease! The smoking lamp is lit."

Red, John, and Bubba looked at one another with bewildered expressions on their faces.

"I never knew it would be like this," Bubba whispered.

"Me, neither. Shit! What have we got ourselves into?" replied Red.

"That Sergeant Kohn must be six-five. Did you see that scar on his face?"

"What have we got ourselves into?" parroted John.

"That Bear guy looks crazy."

"Cottonmouths and alligators." They definitely had John's attention.

"Hey, Driggins," Bubba whispered. "Did you know it would be like this?"

"My daddy was a Marine. He told me what to expect. It ain't too bad once we get in shape. All that hollerin' an' stuff is part of our training."

"You hear that, John Boy? We'll make it OK."

Johnson, a muscular black man spoke up. "My granddaddy was in the Pacific. This place ain't nothin' compared to them days."

Red smiled at his new playmates. "I sure as hell hope not."

Chapter Twelve

Parade Field

"Goddamnit! You there! Get in step. To the rear…March! Close it up! Close it up! Johnson! Hold that standard straight! By the right flank…March! To the rear…March! The rear…March! The rear…March! By the left flank…March! Platoon…Halt! At ease! Atten-hut! Present Arms!"

Sergeant Kohn started down the middle row of the platoon for rifle inspection. There were five rows with fifteen men to each row. He stopped before a suntanned, redheaded recruit from Nebraska. "What's your name, boy?"

"Sir, Private Jones, Sir."

Sergeant Kohn snapped the rifle from Private Jones's hands, flipping it around expertly to look inside the breech. "Private Jones here knows how to clean a weapon. Where'd you learn to do that, Private Jones."

"Sir, I grew up on a farm, Sir."

The Drill Instructor handed back the rifle smartly, then moved past the next man standing at stark attention. He stopped before a tall, slightly pear-shaped individual wearing glasses. "What's your name, Private Four Eyes?"

"Sir, Pasamenus, sir."

"Sir, Private Pasamenus, Sir. Say it right!"

"Sir, Private Pasamenus, Sir."

"Where you from, Private Four Eyes?"

"Sir, Armenia, Sir."

"Why'd you join the Marines, Private Four Eyes?"

"Sir, my parents escaped from the Nazis, Sir. They escaped from the communists too. Sir, I joined to fight the communists, Sir."

Sergeant Kohn reached out and ripped off a loose button from the pocket of Pasamenus's fatigue jacket. "You people listen up. All buttons will be properly secured at all times. Sew that back on when you're in squad bay tonight, Private."

The DI moved on to his next victim. "Them boots is scuffed, boy." He snapped the rifle from the startled recruit's hands. "Holy Mother a Christ! Looks like a nest uh crotch crickets livin' in there." Bubba and Red both snickered.

"Who tha fuck laughed! Who laughed on my parade? Whooo done it?"

Realizing the whole platoon might be in for it, Bubba confessed before Red could open his mouth. "Sir, I did, Sir.

Sergeant Kohn strode around to the front of his platoon. "Front and center, Laughing Boy."

Bubba double-timed from the middle row up before his DI and snapped to attention.

"Where you from, Laughing Boy?

"Sir, Tennessee, Sir."

"Tennessee! Trailer trash whores and barefoot drunks! You got a name, Laughing Boy?"

"Sir, Private Smith, Sir."

"Private Smith here thinks he's a comedian. We got special treatment for your kind, Private Smith. Give me fifteen laps around the platoon. Port Arms! Count 'em off each time you pass the flag-bearer. Move out!

"Riiight face! Fah-ward…March!"

"One!" Bubba rounded the front of the platoon as the other seventy-four trainees marched to Sergeant Kohn's cadence count.

"Hut tup a-rip four! Hut tup a-rip four!"

Five weeks into the program and Platoon 43 was beginning to resemble a competent unit. The men were getting into shape and gaining confidence in themselves, as well as in one another. Most of them could do five to ten pull-ups and fifty to seventy-five sit-ups.

"Two!" Bubba rounded the standard-bearer a second time as they marched across the parade ground in the noonday sun.

"Hut tup a-rip four! Hut tup a-rip four!"

"Three!"

"Double time…March!"

Chapter Thirteen

John's Reoccurring Dream

All had been grand and little boy things until the fifth grade. Then someone up the line decided it would be a feather in their bureaucratic cap to slice the population pie down the middle of Chapman Highway. Sending all the kids on the north side to Galbraith Elementary and the leftovers on the south side to Mooreland Heights would relieve a slight crowding condition at the Galbraith school. It also meant that the Brown's Mountain Barefoot Brigade were forever excommunicated from the ranks of the fine bourgeois children living on the north side of Chapman Highway. The faceless specimens behind this slick maneuver never considered any bad effects on the hapless youngsters soon to be shuffled into an environment resembling divorce. Lifelong playmates were left behind as a New Order sprang up to confront and confound these lobotomized innocents. Tiny scars concealed within were of no consequence to the local school board authorities. Nor did his mother and father fully realize the extent of his personal calamity.

And so it came to pass. Unknown faces resembling gargoyle

masks in an alien classroom, staring back at the small, tassel-haired intruder. A pale, frightened silhouette standing inside the classroom doorway. Who is he? What is he doing here? the children wondered. He felt the ice spider web beneath his feet. Perhaps if he closed his eyes and prayed? Unfathomed expressions engulfed him. Pink, staring faces pulling him down beneath himself, releasing no clue to their acceptance or denial. Why me? he wondered miserably. His first public execution. Tormented he was, as if the whole world, his world, had balanced at the apex of self-pity, waiting for some cosmic sign of deliverance. But God was fresh out of signs that particular day for little boys of ten who longed for their mothers. All fell silent, except for the constant din of sunshine against the windowpanes, and the faint opera of the birds outside.

The teacher was addressing her charges in deference to their welcome newcomer, but he didn't care or even bother to listen. His disgruntled mind was on the other side of Chapman Highway. His social barrier. Earlier that morning he had boarded his old school bus, hoping to slip through. Praying for a miracle. Deliverance. But the fifth-grade instructor turned him away, saying he must obey the rules and go to Mooreland Heights. The rules! His first encounter with The System. Unconditional Surrender. An unseen force bending him to its lobotomized will, tearing him away from the tender womb of childhood. He stood alone for the last time in the center of his cherished playground as the tears slid down his cheeks and fell in tiny pearls to the dusty earth below. There was nothing left to do. The principal had summoned his father.

But instead of the family automobile arriving like always before in John's repetitive nightmare, a military limousine pulled up. Little Johnny opened the door to get in. Seated behind the steering wheel was Sergeant Dipano, wearing a dress blue uniform. In the back seat sat Sergeant Bear and Sergeant Kohn. They, too, were dressed in their official USMC uniforms.

"Get in, Jarhead." Little Johnny does as he's told. "We're going to see the elephant."

John jerked awake. It was 4:55 a.m. Five minutes to go before they had to shit, shine, shave, shampoo, and shower. Then march to the chow hall for breakfast.

Bubba in the top bunk felt John's abrupt departure from dreamland. "What tha hell you doin' down there?"

"I had that dream again. But this time the DIs were in the car."

"Stop dreamin' that shit. You'll end up a Section Eight."

"What you reckon it means? Them DIs an all?"

"Dream about Sam. We belong to the Corps now."

At chow hall, John broached the subject again. "You know, always before I dreamed my father came and got me. This time it was Dipano, Kohn, and Sergeant Bear. They said something about seeing the elephant. I don't know nothin' 'bout no elephants."

Bubba turned to Pasamenus, sitting beside them at the table. "Brain, why do you think he's dreamin' about Drill Sergeants?" Members of the platoon had begun addressing the educated Armenian as the Brain.

"Tell me your dream, John." Private Pasamenus spoke proper English. He was proud to be an American citizen and wise beyond his nineteen years. John described having to change schools in the fifth grade, how he got caught and turned back, and having to call his father to come pick him up. Then he asked Pasamenus about the elephant.

"What exactly do you remember about the elephant?"

"We were going to see one. That's all I remember."

"Your subconscious is talking to you, John. 'Seeing the elephant' is an old expression from many centuries ago, possibly during the time of Hannibal and his elephants. He fought Rome in the Second Punic War, using elephants. During the First World War, the soldiers on both sides referred to 'seeing the elephant' as seeing the face of war. Going into battle. Dreams can mean many things. Some people believe they recall the past. Others believe they foretell the future."

"That's a mouthful, but I never heard about no elephants before."

"Perhaps you read it in a book someplace or overheard someone say it in passing."

"John the fortuneteller." Red was amused.

Pasamenus flashed his friendly Armenian smile. "Yes, John, you may be our fortuneteller."

John laughed. "OK, here goes. Six weeks from now we all graduate from Parris Island. We get a week's leave to go home, eat pogey bait and mama's home cookin'. I'll be with my beautiful wife Sam. The rest a you yard birds will be shackin' up with road whores and God knows what else. Then we travel to our assigned duty stations. The lucky ones will go to Germany or California, England or Australia. Others will get shipboard assignments, maybe on aircraft carriers. The rest, poor lads, are going to Viet-by-god-nam. How'd I do, fellas?

Bubba piped in. "You're a by-god natural, ole son!"

Everybody laughed.

Chapter Fourteen

"This is your rifle..."

The Rifle Range

The M-16 rifle was a 5.56 mm lightweight, air-cooled, gas-operated, magazine-fed, shoulder- or hip-fired weapon designed for automatic or semiautomatic fire. Effective range was 215 yards (200 meters). Magazines came in 20- and 30-round clips. The 5.56 mm was the equivalent of a .223 caliber, as compared with the more powerful .30 caliber bullet of the M-1 rifle used during World War Two and Korea.

The M-16 replaced the M-14 rifle on orders from Secretary of Defense Robert Strange McNamara. Military brass disagreed with his decision. The M-14 was more powerful, firing the NATO 7.62 mm round. It held a 15-round magazine but was considered by McNamara's Whiz Kids as unwieldy in the jungles of Vietnam due to its length and weight. It was also difficult to hold the M-14 on target when firing full automatic due to its more powerful 7.62 mm recoil. But it had superior penetrating power in the dense jungles of Vietnam. An expert rifleman could nail a target at 600 yards.

The M-16 began replacing the M-14 in 1966. Replacements were completed by the end of 1968. M-16 ammunition weighed less, so 30 to 40 percent more ammo could be carried by the average soldier. But many of the veterans viewed the M-16 as a Mattel toy. A poodle shooter. They preferred the heavier and more powerful M-14 assault rifle.

The Russian AK-47, like the American M-14, fired 7.62 mm ammunition. It was heavier than the newer and lighter M-16s, louder, and with considerably more recoil. But the AK-47 was considered more reliable than the M-16s by American troops in the field because of its ability to continue firing when dirty. M-16s often jammed when subjected to dirt or sand. This jamming effect cost the lives of a number of American and Allied soldiers.

"This is your rifle." Sergeant Dipano held up an M-14 in the air. "This is your gun." He grabbed his crotch. "This is for fighting." M-14 in the air. "This is for fun." A girl's best friend. "This week you will learn the manly art of killing commie rat bastards at 200, 300, and 500 yards. You will clean your rifle every day. You will police your brass every time you leave the firing line. You will love your rifle the same as you love your own mother. In return, your rifle will protect you from commie rat bastards. This is what the Marine Corps is all about, ladies. I expect nine experts this week."

Fifteen human silhouettes, from the waist up, rose above the concrete bunkers on pulleys, resembling black and white specters from the underworld. Half the platoon were down in the bunkers to pull and mark targets. The other half remained back on the firing line. After gunnery practice they switched group positions and started all over again.

On the firing line there was one gunnery instructor for every two recruits. His job was to assist the young Marines and make certain they didn't shoot one another. He instructed them about rifle safety, loading their weapons correctly, sight adjustments, and squeezing the trigger slowly so they never knew exactly when the rifle was going to fire.

Kentucky windage was important (leading a target to compensate for any wind). What to do with a misfire, plus a dozen other tricks of the trade. It was imperative that all Marines know their weapons as well as they knew their guns.

"All ready on the right. All ready on the left. All ready on the firing line. Lock and load."

John's first shot was high in the two ring and left about 12 inches. The instructor told him to raise his rear sight aperture two clicks. Then move it three clicks left. His next two shots were low and right in the inside corner of the four ring.

"Bring it one click right. Adjust the weapon in your shoulder. Place the target on top of your front sight. Take a deep breath. Let it halfway out. Then squeeze one off."

His next shot was centered in the five ring.

John Jackson was a natural with the M-14 assault weapon. So was Robert Smith. Having been hunters as youngsters in the woodlands and fields of Tennessee gave them an edge over the others who didn't grow up around shotguns and rifles. It afforded most Southern boys an advantage over their Northern counterparts. Several had a tough time adjusting to their weapons. A few got their thumbs caught in the breech. Others managed purple bruises under their right eyes by not holding the rifle butts tight in against their shoulders. But after awhile everyone got the hang of it. The rifle range resembled a holiday from the rigorous training of boot camp. All of them wanted to make marksman, and especially, expert rifleman.

Fourth day on the range, Bubba and John were down in the bunker pulling targets. Pasamenus and Johnson and First Squad were down there with them. Second Squad was over in the middle. Third Squad was down on the end. Four, Five, and Six Squads were back 300 yards on the firing line. An electrical storm formed out in the Atlantic and blew in over the rifle range. The men on the line were taken indoors for protection against the lightning. The guys down in the bunker huddled together under a rebar reinforced concrete overhang which sheltered them from the rain.

A bolt of lightning struck the ground directly behind the bunker. First squad felt a slight tingling sensation. Next thing they knew, a couple of water moccasins as big around as a man's arm came slithering over the rear wall, landing on both sides of Johnson who was sitting with his back against the front wall snoozing. Insomnia was never a problem at Parris Island. The muscular black man opened his eyes when he heard the sound of the snakes, but before he could acknowledge his dire predicament, Pasamenus stepped in front him holding a broken wooden pole for signaling shooters back on the firing line.

"Don't Move!" Pasamenus spoke with authority. "Don't Move, Marcus!"

Marcus Johnson glanced down. He saw them coiled and ready to strike. Johnson closed his eyes and remained motionless. With his wooden stick, Pasamenus enticed the snake nearest him to strike. The instant it did, he spun his pole around catching the snake in the midsection and flipping it out the open end of the bunker. Then he performed the same procedure with the second cottonmouth.

Johnson stumbled to his feet with an unbelieving look on his face. "Where the hell did you learn that?" he asked, pounding Pasamenus on the back until his glasses hung sideways, while shaking his hand up and down like a bunkhouse water pump. "You saved my life!"

"Father managed a circus when I was little. The snake handler did that whenever the cobra got out. He used a cardboard box. You can pin them behind the head, you know. Then you can pick them up. But with two snakes, you were in a fix, so I flipped them out the exit."

The tall Armenian behaved as if nothing unusual had happened. His mother and father had reinforced their young son years before with stories about Nazi atrocities across Europe, and Stalin's gulags and his terrible KGB.

The men of First Squad looked upon Pasamenus differently after the snake episode. The Brain had become more to them than a tall, willowy bookworm. He was brave and a cool customer under fire. Johnson saw him now as a true friend. The powerful black man would shield his friend from harm more than once in the jungles of Southeast Asia.

Next morning was qualification day. Everyone was nervous. A handful were afraid they might not qualify. That meant getting sent back to another platoon. First Squad was confident of qualification, with the exception of Private Henry who was just average at best.

Dwayne Henry came from Manhattan. His daddy was a high-dollar pimp. Mama was poppa's sloe-eyed, mattress-banging sweet thang. So were two bodacious young drug addicts living downstairs in the same hotel. One called himself Samson. The other cocaine-addled lovely, a 20-year-old girl from Kentucky, was known as Delilah. Their specialties were bisexual businessmen down on Wall Street. Two-on-one fast breaks with the smart set over on Park Avenue. And those back door thespians from Broadway were always a smash hit. They entertained Jews, gentiles, men or women. Everybody was welcome up on West 81st Street.

Poppa received fifteen to twenty calls a week for Samson and Delilah. They were a vaudevillian triumph every time they performed the nasty. And the talk of the town among the upper crust who relished something a little different from those they promised to love, cherish, and obey. But mama was poppa's ace in the hole. Men became addicted to her between-the-sheets piece de resistance as a sexual superstar. Mama and the two hedonists downstairs were poppa's tribute to genteel living. Poppa never worked a day in his life.

Dwayne prayed over every meal. The Catholic Church had become his sanctuary in the Big Apple. "His home away from Satan's parlor," Father McCreary once told him. Dwayne had joined the Marines to get away from mama and poppa and their lifestyle of debauchery. He didn't smoke or drink. He didn't curse or gamble or do the dirty deed with women. Dwayne was a devout believer in Jesus Christ. The men thought him quaint but accepted him as a good-natured Bible thumper. The DIs called him Private Gideon. Dwayne Henry took it all in stride. He was proud to be a Marine.

His first shot was a Maggie's drawers. A miss. His next nine shots were all over the target. Threes and fours and a single bull's-eye. Before his next ten rounds his range instructor knelt down beside him.

"Son, look down at the grass a few seconds before you shoot. It helps clear the vision. Now think about Jesus Christ up there on that cross. He died for your sins. The least you can do for Him is to qualify as a Marine Corps rifleman."

Dwayne Henry qualified rifleman that day on the rifle range with four points to spare.

Bubba qualified expert rifleman. Pasamenus fired high expert. Johnson, Red, and two other recruits also qualified as expert rifleman. All 75 Marines qualified rifleman or better, but John drew the attention of his Drill Instructors by firing an amazing 244 out of a possible 250. When Platoon 43 marched back to their barracks, those seven recruits were held back at the rifle range for two extra days of target practice. Their instructors gave them M-14 rifles fitted with long-range telescopic sights. Sniper rifles. After the first day, each man could place a 7.62 round through the bull's-eye at 600 yards. By the time they rejoined their platoon two days later they could center the target at one thousand yards.

Chapter Fifteen

Bivouac

Suited up with a twenty-pound pack on his back, boots, rifle, cartridge belt, canteen, bayonet, helmet, and a pack of Marlboros, John was ready to roll. Platoon 43 was assembled in front of their barracks at 1500 hours. Sergeant Dipano, Sergeant Bear, and Sergeant Kohn presiding.

"You people got a record to beat today. Five miles in 53 minutes. Old record is 54 minutes. That means you gotta hump it. No stragglers. No breaks. No pogey bait Marines. Blisters ain't no excuse. Flake out and we'll sell your ass to the locals for gator bait. I want them 53 minutes, people."

Jogging in platoon formation their first mile went pretty well. Then someone stumbled in Fourth Squad and fell, causing half a dozen to go down behind him. The Drill Instructors swarmed like hornets.

"Get up, ya herd a monkeys! Up! Up! Close it up! Close it up!"

The second mile was more difficult. With boots and the rest of their paraphernalia, they were lugging close to forty pounds. Jogging on sand was similar to running in loose dirt, their boots kept sliding in the sand. And the canvas straps on their packs chaffed their shoulders, rubbing off the skin. Gravity and the weight of the rifles tugged at their forearms until their muscles ached and burned.

By the third mile they were soaked with sweat from head to toe. Another man stumbled and fell, four more behind him sprawled down in the sand. "Get up! Get up! Close it up! Close it up, people!"

Midway through their fourth mile, Sergeant Bear called a twenty-second break. "Drink a mouthful of water. Tighten your packs. Take deep breaths. Ignore the pain. We're almost there. Move out, men. Close it up. Close it up."

With a mile to go they were straggling badly, strung out 200 feet along the trail. Muscles aching, the raw places on their shoulders bathed with their own sweat stung like crazy. They weren't going to beat any records. It was too damn hard.

Sergeant Dipano pushed their buttons. "You fucks want the Island to hear about this? How a bunch a Navy Seal assholes beat our people? They're the ones with them 54 minutes. You call yourselves Leathernecks? Horse Shit! My granny could beat you pussies with a locker box on her head! This is by-god pathetic! I don't think you people pack the gear! Want me to call the trucks to come get your candy asses? One fucking mile is all you need. One stinking-ass mile to beat the chicken-shit Navy! CAN YOU DO IT?"

Johnson howled first. "Gung Ho!"

Red took up the cry. "Gung Ho, Mother Fucker! Gung Ho!"

They ran like wild beasts, lungs heaving for oxygen, shoulder straps chaffing raw flesh, blisters burst and bleeding. They ran like savages, legs awkward and flailing out, white-eyed with exhaustion. They ran with threads of spittle hanging from their gaping mouths. They ran in a world of pain and determination and guts and glory. They ran because they were United States Marines.

When the last man staggered across the five-mile marker and collapsed in the sand, they had beaten the record set by the Navy Seals by 49 seconds. Their Drill Instructors praised them for the first time at Parris Island. It was a marvelous feeling. Some laughed and shook hands. Others yelled and hollered. Some were just glad to still be alive. They bivouacked that night in the boondocks, ate C rations for supper, then fell asleep beneath their combined shelter halves. There were plenty enough mosquitoes to go around for everybody. Next morning, the trucks came and hauled them back to their barracks. Sick Bay dispensed the usual salve and aspirin. They were proud of their achievement. They had beaten the Navy's best.

Chapter Sixteen

Graduation

Thirteen weeks of unprecedented ball-busting, in-your-face, whup-ass hell had transformed a mangy herd of seventy-five pogey bait civilians, mama's boys all, loopy in the head and soft in the middle, into a crack platoon of jarhead sumbitches you didn't wanna mess with. Pasamenus had gone from a shmoo-shaped bookworm to one lean and lanky hard-nosed intellectual. Johnson and Bubba had gained eight pounds apiece, which made their 215-pound frames more than a little intimidating. John had shed his 90 proof love handles and was in the best shape of his life. They were all like that. Dwayne Henry had taken his pledge as a US Marine with the same devotion a bridegroom addresses his wedding vows. He loved the Corps. Red looked ferocious with his muscular arms and piercing green eyes.

To many of them it didn't seem possible that boot camp was almost over. It was physically the hardest thing any of them had ever accomplished. Football didn't compare with Parris Island. Football players go home after football practice, eat pogey bait, and watch television. Boot camp was 24 hours a day, minus about seven hours for sleeping. Mentally, it had altered their psyches. All that hounding and harassment didn't seem quite so bad in hindsight. It was all part of their conditioning. Nothing personal, but without the mental plus the physical, that fine razor's edge could never be attained which makes the Marine Corps the finest fighting machine on earth. It molds the men, the few, the brave. The ones who strike fear in the hearts of commie rat bastards.

It was a clear day without a cloud in the South Carolina sky. A soft autumn breeze made the parade grounds a comfortable setting for the big send off. Most of the sand fleas were away on holiday. Overhead, an armada of sea gulls performed a flyover, lending their support to the official proceedings. Wooden bleachers had been set up for the two dozen or so parents who came to watch their sons graduate. Some of the Island's brass were present, colonels, majors, captains. But the individual who caught everyone's eye was the old general with all the ribbons on his chest, making his way up to the podium. Platoon 43 stood at attention awaiting his speech. Sergeant Dipano, Kohn, and Bear stood proudly in front of their seventy-five charges.

Johnson glanced over at Pasamenus. "Pretty cool, man."

"Yes," whispered Pasamanus. "Today we become Marines."

The general mounted the stage and began to speak. At first it was the usual stuff about pride in one's self, pride in the Corps, a great history to uphold, sacrifice for God and country, but then it began to change.

"You men are the vanguard against a dark and uncertain future. An ill wind is blowing through the political capitals of the world. Communism is on the march again. I'm retiring the end of this month so I'm going to express my personal opinion here today. Winston Churchill warned the free world about an Iron Curtain descending across Europe in the days following World War Two. A senator from Wisconsin by the name of Joseph McCarthy warned our nation against communists in our own government back in the 1950s. Turns out Churchill and McCarthy were both right. Now we're fighting another war against communism, in Vietnam. So far, Washington and our Pentagon aren't doing a very good job. Damned lousy job, as a matter of fact.

"New leadership is needed to persevere against the forces of evil. It will be up to you young men, and men and women like you, to protect and serve this great nation until that new leadership can be found. What this country needs is patriotic men and women with vision and fortitude to lead us out of these dark days of political appeasement and indecision, and into a new dawn of hope and spiritual prosperity.

"Today you officially become United States Marines. Many good men and women have gone on before you. Some made the supreme sacrifice. Many more will follow in your footsteps. War is a tough business. War is Marine Corps business. That is the reason our training is hard and disciplined. You learned things here that will guide you when situations in the field come into question. Always conduct yourselves as gentlemen. Always be a credit to the uniform. But make no mistake about it, Marines. You are now trained, professional killers."

The platoon was dismissed and most of the men headed back to their barracks. Excitement was in the air. They were going home on leave. But a few of the men held back. They had things they wanted to say to their Drill Instructors. Private Driggins was the first to approach Sergeant Dipano. Sergeant Kohn and Sergeant Bear looked on with interest, not knowing what to expect.

Private Driggins held out his hand. "Sir, may I shake your hand, Sir?"

Sergeant Dipano was a short, stocky Italian with black hair and black eyes who had been sent back to the States because of wounds received in Vietnam. His stern face broke into a smile. "Sure thing, son. I'd be honored."

Then the others crowded in and shook hands all around. Sergeant Bear laughed and didn't appear quite so terrible after all. Sergeant Kohn then placed his large hands on the shoulders of each man, one after another, speaking to them in a solemn voice.

"It was the custom among the chiefs of my tribe to lay their hands on the shoulders of the young braves before they went into battle. This is the Indian sign for bravery passed down from the Great Spirit. Some of you are going into combat. The rest of you will serve those men fighting. These are my words. Where ever you go, I wish each one of you good health and good fortune. And always, good hunting."

Private Henry had tears in his eyes. Private Pasamenus knew in his heart that his destiny was being fulfilled. They felt a kinship toward their Drill Instructors, a fierceness of loyalty they had never known before. John stood staring at the big Cherokee and the long white scar down his face. And remembering, too, what the general had said about the Marines being the vanguard against communism, and about him and Bubba being professional killers. A chill passed over his body as though someone had walked across his grave.

Bubba punched his arm. "Come on, man, let's go. It's time for chow."

The bus ride back to Knoxville took forever. Or so it seemed. John couldn't wait to see Samantha, and Bubba had a hot date with Suzie Brown.

Chapter Seventeen

Furlough

At 10:15 p.m., after sixteen miserable hours, they disembarked their bus from sunny Parris Island. The Trailways station at Gay and Main in Knoxville never looked so good.

The old courthouse across Main Street brought back fond memories for John. Sam and him running up those eight marble steps to get their marriage license, then running back down. She'd tripped, and John had caught her before she fell.

Both men remembered the city jail a block south on Gay Street at the corner of Hill Avenue. They certainly had visited that place a time or two. All that was history now. Another lifetime. Another world ago. Even getting married seemed in the distant past. So much had happened since their wild and woolly days as a couple of lost balls in the high weeds.

Bubba and John had drawn Vietnam as their duty assignments. So had the rest of Platoon 43. Other platoons from their graduation ceremony had been dispersed all over the globe. Camp Pendleton, Germany, Japan, Hawaii, shipboard duty in the Pacific. It was exciting. They all knew Americans were being killed in Vietnam. It was splattered all over the six o'clock news every night with the Huntley-Brinkley Report and Walter Cronkite.

That didn't bother them much. Each time he spoke on TV, President Johnson assured the American people that progress was being made. General Westmoreland explained his strategy for containing the North, while fighting the war in the jungles of South Vietnam. We were winning. Commie rat bastards were losing. Hooray for our side. But the antiwar movement continued.

John hadn't written Samantha when exactly he would be coming home. The sly dog played it cool. Private Jackson wanted to surprise his blushing bride. Sam loved surprises, so John was bringing her one.

Suzie already knew when Bubba would be there. She was waiting at the bus station to pick them up. Suzie had trimmed down several pounds and looked stunning. Having graduated cosmetology school, she was working full time at a swank beauty salon in West Knoxville. Finally, she was free from the life she hated. Being poor.

Her allure as a big-breasted knockout was a valuable asset in the professional world of hairstyles, perfume, and gay caballeros. The gay crowd loved Suzie. Everyone liked her. Her commonsense earthiness and sweet disposition made her a star. She had acquired an apartment in Sequoyah Village and a red Ford Mustang. As the boys were getting off the bus, she ran to greet them.

"Bubba! John! Welcome home, guys!"

She dashed into Bubba's arms and kissed him. Then she turned to John and kissed him on the cheek. The two Marines gaped at their old gangbang queen in awe and amazement. It was a year and a half since John had seen her. More than a year for Bubba. Stylishly dressed in a miniskirt with all the necessary fashion accoutrements, her shoulder-length auburn hair radiated sparkling highlights she had learned in the beauty trade. Manicured nails and eyebrows, sensual blue eye shadow, cherry red lipstick. Bubba's mouth hung open. Suzie was drop-dead gorgeous. She smelled good too.

"Damn, Suzie!" John held her at arm's length. "You're beautiful!"

Bubba followed his lead. "I done died and gone to Beulah Land."

Suzie teased back. "I bet you boys say that to all the girls. You do, don't you?"

Everyone burst out laughing, each silently remembering their stone quarry escapades. Suzie had changed, much the same as John and Bubba had changed. She had respect now, and dignity, something she never realized before. Suzie was happy with her new life. And she had a date with a "college boy"! The two Marines retrieved their duffle bags from the luggage compartment, then walked Suzie to her car.

It was an affectionate reunion motoring out Alcoa Highway to deliver John to Samantha. They reminisced about the old days, when John was bombed half the time and Robert was bumfuzzled over life. The men weren't going to mention the stone quarry, but Suzie brought up the subject anyway.

"About the stone quarry…," she began. Neither one responded, so she continued. "It's OK, guys. We had our fun back then, but there's something I want to ask you. Please don't mention it to Samantha. She comes in the shop now and then. I don't want her to know about any of that. I like her. We've become friends."

"The past is past, Suzie." Bubba patted her arm.

"We were crazy as bedbugs back then." John smiled at her in the rearview mirror. "Your secrets are safe with me and Jarhead up there."

"Semper Fi, Suzie, baby." Bubba was in awe of the beautiful lady driving the Mustang.

They arrived at the little house on Edison Street a few minutes before eleven. John unloaded his duffle bag from the trunk, lugged it up the sidewalk, and knocked on the front door. A porch light came on. Sam appeared in the doorway, wearing hair curlers and a housecoat.

Bubba and Suzie waved good-bye and drove away.

Bubba couldn't get over how pretty Suzie looked. She was so different from before that he thought maybe he should ask her to take him back to his parents' place.

Suzie reached for Bubba's hand. "Honey, can you stay with me tonight?"

Samantha shrieked with happiness. She dragged John into the living room and planted a big wet one right on the kisser. They stood close holding one another, their hearts beating together as one. Words were not necessary. Sam took John's Marine jacket, hung it on a chair, then pulled him down beside her on the couch, loosened his tie, and kissed him again.

"I love you, Samantha. I've always loved you."

"Oh, Johnny, you're going to make me cry."

"Don't you start blubbering 'cause I might too."

"Isn't this wonderful? I never knew two people could be this happy."

"You're perfect Sam, in every way. You're my Eve."

"And you're my Adam. A big handsome Marine I adore."

"I have eight days before I go back. Eight glorious days."

"Take your things off, baby. I want you right here on the sofa."

"Would you like to have a baby, Sam?"

"Yes, my darling. Two or three, maybe."

John didn't have to be asked twice. He obeyed like a well-disciplined Marine. She pulled off her housecoat and panties, then straddled her man, facing him…easing down gently, taking him inside her tender wetness. She rode her Marine like he was a stallion. Pure Ecstasy!

Samantha devoured John's face with her lips, her tongue, digging her nails into his neck and shoulders, his arms. "Oh, Johnny, I love you so much."

John clasped his hands around Sam's bouncing bottom and held on for dear life. Afterward, Samantha broke out a bottle of Brut champagne she'd been saving for the occasion. Champagne always tickled her nose but she liked the stuff anyway. They hugged again and again. John kissed her face, her breasts, her tummy. With a champagne glow lighting the way, they make love a second time.

"Sammy, oh, Sammy."

Sam held him close, savoring their union, her legs locked around his waist until John delivered his seed.

"What Becomes of the Broken Hearted" began playing on the radio. Red's favorite tune by Jimmy Ruffin. Something about the song piqued John's interest. He disengaged from Samantha's sleepy arms and turned up the volume a little. Then he snuggled down beside her again.

The words drifted out of the darkness, settling over him like pieces of a puzzle. In his semi state of Morpheus, John remembered Red's sadness over the loss of Carolyn, and his own misery while separated from Samantha. Two events had turned his life around, Sam and the Marine Corps. Where would he be if Samantha were not his bride? What would life serve up if Red and Bubba and the Corps were not part of his future? Drowsily he reached out a hand to touch his wife and reassure himself that she was real and not an illusion.

The elephant burst out of the darkness in a horrible vision. A monstrous beast of war, slavering and wild-eyed, thundering through the jungle, smashing everything in its path while the wail of air-raid sirens cried in the distance. The dreaded Apollyon. A vassalage to evil. Then it transformed into the Reaper, a horrid thing in black robes, swinging a great scythe. Harvesting souls. Striding above the carnage of war, hunting, searching, venting its venomous rage, leering down at its subjects below as one views maggots feasting on a rotting corpse. Skulls littered a lunar landscape. Everywhere there were flames and destruction and human suffering. And beyond it all, on a distant dark horizon, a flood of white crosses cascading up into a crimson sky.

"No!" He cried out. "No! No!"

Samantha awakened and held him, fear in her frightened eyes. "Oh, John. My poor, sweet John."

John never told Samantha about his dream. He brushed it off as pre-Vietnam jitters. Instead, they made the most of the time they had together, driving through the Smoky Mountains, picnics on the riverbanks in Rockford and Louisville, hiking a three-mile trail in Townsend, visiting with their parents and, of course, The Paris Café.

Angelina prepared a special cocktail for them their first night back. Cosmopolitan, she called it. They toasted Angelina, themselves, and the USMC. Three cosmopolitans. Whatever she put in them was a mite strong. They were up until two in the morning huggy bear and kissy facing.

Chapter Eighteen

Down Under

Bubba called their third day back. He and Suzie wanted John and Samantha to join them at a new club downtown.

"It's a place called The Down Under. It's downstairs in the old Farragut Hotel. Some guy by the name of Morton runs it. Suzie's been there and says it's great."

"OK, we'll see you there around 7:30. Sam takes an hour to get dressed, anyway."

"I heard that, mister. No snuggles for you tonight!"

Bubba listened to them laughing. "We'll see ya there, dude."

The Down Under was a cool place for the affluent, as well as folks with a few bucks in their jeans. Susan Preston, the most sought-after femme fatale in Knoxville, made her grand debuts on Friday nights. Peter Athas was an artist and the darling of the smart set. He catered the scene for inspiration and the occasional damsel in need of "artistic appreciation." Pete's sidekick and budding novelist, Michael Henry, dropped by on occasion for the camaraderie and to acquire profiles for his next book. A nubile society princess, Nannette Fanning, made appearances on a regular basis to meet Beau Brummells. Nannette enjoyed getting her ashes hauled, as did most everyone else during the heady reign of the sexual revolution. Politicians drifted in and out. Dave Troutman was often present. And Deke Brackett with his merry band of West Knox Patchers were usually in attendance. It was a grand environment for having a down-home get together. The dance floor was rocking, the patrons were in the groove, and the booze was always plentiful. Barrister Lockridge was pontificating at the bar this evening beside his lovely bride Anne and a jubilant group of courtroom magicians, plus one intoxicated judge, on the subject of "Mama and the Old South."

"I'm old now but I remember Mama.
She was tha purtiest one.
Comin' down tha stairs in her pearls an crinolin gowns
Mama had tha bestest parties in tha whole county
An' there was Poppa
Always ridin' high ta tha hounds
Smellin' uh leath-ah an good Kentucky bourbon
It's all gone now... alllll gone
'Ceptin' Poppa's leath-ah saddle
An Mama's yellow verbena douche bag."

Lieutenant Paul met with his group at the bar near the front door. Bill, John, and Bubba pounded one another on the back like long-lost brothers, while Sam and Suzie lit out for the ladies room for a nose-powdering session. There was much ado about Parris Island, the Marine Corps, Smoke and Mirrors Land, and Vietnam. Bill spotted Susan Preston sitting at a table and asked if anyone knew her. Bubba did, from UT, so he went over and asked if they might join her table.

Extra chairs were produced and the evening took flight.

"So, pretty lady, what do you do for a living?"

"I'm a real estate agent. My father helps me out with leads."

"Must be nice, all mine left me was a steamer trunk."

"What was in it?" she asked.

"Just junk. Letters from me. Letters from my mother. His service records in the Merchant Marines. A dress uniform, some old clothes, and a pistol from Germany."

"He loved you. That's why he kept those things."

Bill Paul gazed back at Susan Preston in a new light. No one had ever said that before. He knew it to be true, but he choked up on it just the same. He turned his head aside, as if to clear his throat, to conceal his misty vision.

John chimed in. "Why don't you guys dance? Me an' Sam's gonna cut a rug."

They all flocked to the dance floor. Bubba and Suzie. Samantha and John. Bill and Susan. "I've Been Loving You Too Long" was playing by Otis Redding.

Freddie Morton, the owner, was friends with Susan Preston. He approached their table with a tray of fresh drinks. "Here ya go, folks, compliments of the house."

Susan turned to Bill and clinked glasses. "Here's to you, Bill Paul."

Walnut Ridge Country Club was owned and operated by Earl McMillan. Earl owned several business interests around Knoxville, including an excavating company in Lenoir City. Suzie had contacted John's father, Frank, who was friends with Mister McMillan. Her idea was to throw a surprise going away party for the boys at Walnut Ridge. Mister Jackson thought it was a splendid idea.

Earl McMillan was too young for World War One and he never got drafted in the Second World War because of his age, but his father had served with Teddy Roosevelt and the Rough Riders during the

Spanish American War. Earl was a patriot. He and most of his generation had lost friends and relatives in those hard fought battles with the Japanese and Nazi Germany. Earl was only too happy to arrange John and Bubba a send-off party.

Mister and Missus Jackson conspired with Mister and Missus Smith, Suzie, Samantha, Miss Martha, and Mister McMillan to arrange a "dinner" at Walnut Ridge the night before the boys were to catch their flight for California. They were sad and fretful over their sons, and they wanted to do something special for them before they went away. Mister Smith chartered a limousine to accommodate all eleven members in one vehicle so they would arrive together.

When they walked into the main ballroom where the lighted fish tank separated the back bar area from the rear dance floor, Bubba and John were greeted by Bill Rutherford's band playing and fifty guests on their feet singing "Dixie." Besides John's marriage and Bubba falling head over heels for Suzie, that was the happiest moment of their lives.

Red and his family were out of town visiting his grandparents in Crystal River, Florida.

Mister McMillan took the microphone and welcomed everyone onboard. Brown Trucking was represented by Tom and Roy Brown. Lloyd and Katharine Morris with Jack Marshal and lovely bride Jackie were in attendance for General Tire. Congressman Johnny Butler and his wife Priscilla were sitting beside Mister and Missus Jackson. Bob and Pauline Sams from Vestal and Billy and Marguerite Henry from the little grocery store over in Rockford. Wanda and Colonel C.A. Henry. Helen Miller, Jimmy Waller, and Effie Mae Butler. Billy and Dot Sams from South Knoxville. Miss Preston and Lieutenant Paul. Clyde and Lela Butler from Louisville, Tennessee. Hattie Gibson with Saint Mary's Hospital. Friends from high school and college.

Then the former Knox County Register of Deeds, Gordon Sams, took the stage. "Folks, you all know why we're here tonight. Two of Knoxville's finest young men are going away to serve their country in

Vietnam, John Jackson and Robert Smith. We all wish them Godspeed and happy landings. Now, if you'll bow your heads with me I'll say the blessing.

"Dear heavenly Father, two of our boys are leaving here tomorrow morning for Vietnam. We pray that You watch over them and protect them. Just as we pray for the safety and well-being of all our young men and women in uniform. Please bring them back home safely, dear Lord. God bless this food we are about to receive. And God bless America."

After dinner, the band played "Stardust" and the dance floor filled to capacity. It was an evening of enchantment for everyone to remember. Earl McMillan looked on like a proud father. Then Bubba walked up to the stage and asked to use the microphone.

"John and I would like to thank all of you for this wonderful surprise. We couldn't ask for a nicer bunch a folks. Thank you! We really do appreciate this. Now there was something I was going to do when I got back from my tour of duty, but I believe tonight is the best time for it.

"Miss Suzie Elizabeth Brown. Sweetheart, will you marry me?"

Suzie Brown clasped her hands over her mouth, a glad wind filling her sails. She hurried onto the dance floor and stood before Robert with the biggest smile ever. Suzie flung her arms around his neck and kissed him.

"Yes." she said. "Yes, I will." Turning to the audience, "I love this wonderful man."

Applause, whistles, laughter…the band struck up "The Wedding March."

Later that night, in bed, Bubba held Suzie close. "When I get where I'm going, I'll switch my insurance over to your name. Then I'll mail the papers back here. I sure do wish we had time to get you a ring. I'll look around when I get over there, maybe find you something special, OK?"

Suzie pulled herself over on top of Bubba and began to cry.

"Don't cry, baby. I might get leave in six months. We could meet in Hawaii. Think you'd like Hawaii?"

Suzie just blubbered and hugged him. "Please don't get hurt. Please, Bubba. I couldn't stand it if they sent you home in a box."

"I ain't comin' home in no box. Now wipe them tears away and gimme a kiss, ya ole soon-to-be-married sweet thang."

"I love you, Robert. I love you so much it makes me dizzy."

They made love into the wee hours of the morning. Sleep was not on the agenda for either couple that particular evening.

Chapter Nineteen

Coffee Tea or Me

They boarded Delta Flight 11 at 8:10 a.m. at the McGhee Tyson Airport ten miles outside Knoxville. Sam and Suzie hugged them one last time, then kissed them good-bye. The others had said their farewells the evening before. Thus began the first leg of their journey. Vietnam no longer seemed an illusion. Parris Island was fast receding into a long time ago. So were their former lives as civilians. The unreality of it all had come to pass. They were on their way to French Indochina, a place where adventure and death lurked in the shadows. A great uncertainty lay before them and they were each a little afraid for the first time, but still, the mystery and excitement mixed well with their budding concerns.

"Oh, man, I'm sleepy. We were up all night."

"Me too. But wasn't it great, though?" Both men laughed.

"You scared, John?"

"Yeah, I been thinkin' about it all week. I never tell Sam this stuff, but I been havin' these dreams about the jungle. I ain't never seen no jungle before. So I guess I am, a little."

"What kinda dreams?"

"One time I dreamed about a big elephant. You remember at PI when the Brain told us about seein' the elephant? Then I dreamed about, you know, Mister Bones…things like that."

"That's freaky, man."

"I dream weird stuff."

"Remember back when I went to see Bill about your drinkin' an' all?"

"Yeah, what about it?"

"Bill said you and me was different. He said I was country inside, like him. Said you was city inside, that you took things more to heart than some folks. I bet that's why you been havin' them dreams."

"Maybe so. Now am I supposed to call you Pluto Swint or Redneck?"

"Fuck you, City Slicker. Go to sleep."

Two hours out from Knoxville they were passing over a muddy river in Oklahoma. Down below lay a sea of white clouds scattered from horizon to horizon. "Eight Miles High" by The Byrds was playing over the ship's intercom system.

A pretty brunette stewardess knelt down in the aisle beside Bubba's seat and whispered in his ear. "Coffee, tea, or me?" she whispered. He opened his eyes to find a note pressed into his palm.

> *"My name is Marty. The other stew is Alta.*
> *We're staying at the same hotel tonight if you and*
> *your friend would like to join us. Room 310."*

John opened his eyes to see Marty's shapely bottom retreating down the aisle as Bubba passed the note over to him. The lyrics of the song were about a plane trip, then touching down in a strange and unfamiliar country. Somehow the song disturbed John. He wondered again about Vietnam and what mysteries lay in store there for him and Red and Bubba.

Bubba smiled. "A jarhead's dream."

"Yeah…but you ain't goin' are ya?"

"No way. I promised Suzie. But it's good knowin' we still got it, ole buddy."

"I reckon so. Yeah, we do, don't we."

The layover in San Diego turned into a family reunion. No sooner had they squared away their duffle bags and bedded down for some much-needed rest, when the telephone rang.

"Hello, Marine."

"Who is this?"

"Sir, Private Pasamenus, Sir." John burst out laughing. "John, all of First Squad are here in the hotel. We're downstairs in the lounge if you and Bubba would care to join us."

"Give us ten minutes, dude."

Private Pasamenus was seated at the bar beside his friend Private Johnson, both wearing their dress green uniforms. Private Henry and the rest of First Squad were scattered around the room wearing the same getup. The place was filled with Navy and Marines. Wilson Pickett was on the jukebox wailing "In the Midnight Hour" when John and Bubba walked into the smoke-filled watering hole. The two Delta girls from the plane were there. Bubba went over and thanked them for their invitation. The ladies were both impressed and apologetic, not realizing before then that these particular jarheads were spoken for. Then he and John joined their two buddies at booze central and proceeded to toast one another, the USMC, the Navy, and John by-god Wayne.

"I hate fuckin' Marines!"

The four of them turned around to see 250 pounds of badass, decorated with tattoos on both muscular arms and wearing gang colors standing three feet behind them. Bubba started to get up but the biker yanked him off his stool before his feet hit the deck, and knocked him sprawling across the floor. Johnson jumped up and cracked the man hard in the jaw. The biker spat blood, then knocked Johnson across the room where he landed beside Bubba. Before John could get off his stool the biker slammed him ass end over teakettle under the table where the Delta stewardesses were sitting.

"Sir! That is quite enough. I suggest you leave now."

The tattooed monster smirked at Pasamenus, then spat blood in his face. "Fuck you, asshole. I'm jes gettin' cranked up good."

The large man came in fast with a roundhouse delivery. Pasamenus slipped sideways, smartly, creating a miss. With catlike agility the young Marine grabbed the biker's left hand, yanking it into his chest…then snapped the fingers backwards with all his might, the breaking bones made cracking sounds…Biker Boy bellowed in pain and rage, then backed away to reappraise this strange new situation. Pulling out a nasty looking switchblade, he lunged for his quarry. Pasamenus slipped again like the bullfighter…turned sharply, chopping him across the throat with the back edge of his hand…pivoted 360 degrees, delivering an elbow to the solar plexus…then came up beneath the chin with a fierce uppercut. Biker Boy crashed to the hardwood floor, dazed and bleeding, fingers broken, fractured jaw, gasping for breath.

The whole room erupted in applause. Pasamenus retired to his stool and proceeded to wipe the spittle off his face with a towel handed him by the barkeep. The rest of First Squad were standing around with their mouths hanging open in disbelief.

Johnson retrieved the knife from the floor and handed it to Pasamenus. "Thank God you're on our side!"

John could not contain his curiosity. "Let me guess, Brain. You learned that stuff with the circus, right?"

Pasamenus just smiled and sipped his cocktail.

Five o'clock wake-up calls jarred everyone awake from a sound slumber. Cab rides to the airport, a quick breakfast of bacon and eggs, and they were on their way again, this time with 150 fellow Marine and Navy personnel. A hundred miles out over a blue Pacific most of the cast had stolen away to dreamland. It was freezing inside the airplane.

John dreamed about The Byrds, the cold from a malfunctioning air conditioning, and the uncertainty awaiting them on the other side of the world. He dreamed he was stranded on the side of a snow-covered mountain.

…he could remain where he was no longer. It was too dangerous. He had to go higher. Any attempt to climb back down was suicide. Most of the ledge he had been on had broken away and fallen into the abyss. All that remained was a narrow foothold, the sheer granite wall below, and the eerie cry of the wind. The sound reminded him of the wail of lost souls.

He renewed his ascent. When he reached the top he could call for help. There would be a ranger station up there someplace. He was going to be just fine. Mountain climbing was not his cup of tea.

Heavy clouds obscured the summit. If only the wind would settle down so he could hear himself think. He gazed out over a breathtaking panorama, feeling a thrill run down his spine. There, on a precarious ledge at the top of the world, he marveled at the sheer beauty of God's majestic tapestry.

He had never seen anything like it. Maybe climbing mountains wasn't so bad after all. Just so he didn't slip and tumble over the ledge. Getting up this far had been a major accomplishment, something never done before. He felt proud of himself.

The rocks cut his hands. They were slippery from the ice and snow. Stinging pellets of sleet peppered his face. A trickle of blood ran down his ring finger. It was cold. The pain made him more aware of the precipice.

This was scary stuff. What in the world was he doing up here?

Bubba had talked him into this stunt. A guy could get killed waltzing this crazy fandango.

He made it to within a few yards of the clouds. It looked like cotton candy that time at the county fair when he was a boy. He remembered holding his daddy's hand, marveling at all the people around. If only his father were there now to hold his hand once again.

The wind was just tolerable at that elevation, eighteen maybe twenty knots. He was several thousand feet above the tree line. Down below he saw a serpentine river of pewter, and high above, long ribbons of cirrus clouds. An eagle appeared. Off toward the horizon was a tiny village. He thought he could see smoke rising from their chimney pots. Perhaps not, at least they were safe and warm.

Everywhere he looked, purple-and-white wilderness. Jagged fingers of rock pointing up in accusatory fashion toward a multidimensional cosmic universe. He had chosen the highest and toughest peak of all. Man! He really got his money's worth this trip to the five-and-dime. Farther up, he struggled until the clouds took him. Nothing had prepared him for the shadow world he entered. Swirling ghosts, phantoms peering out from gray mists, sunsets from long ago, forgotten dawns. His turbulent youth, a haunted maelstrom of people and events, smelling of burnt ozone.

Thunder broke loudly over the valley behind him, reverberating among the mighty peaks the challenge of Thor. A feeling of awareness descended upon the climber. Instinctively he knew he was not alone. Fear. Shame. Hate. Love. Pride. Were these the beings that inhabit man's soul? Lightning stoked the mountain's rocky crags, momentarily illuminating his fingers like predatory claws.

In that flash of vision, he saw that nothing lived there. No plants, no lichen. It was as though he were climbing a mountain that had no soul. Cobbled isomers in a cerebral vortex. Suspended existence in a land without hope. He halted to catch his breath. The thin atmosphere burned his lungs. Sweat streaked his matted hair, then froze in tattered strands giving him the appearance of an unkempt gargoyle.

Visions of a malignant world gathered inside his head in strobe-light succession resembling the lighted windows of a passenger train passing through the night. Just what I need, he thought numbly. A rerun of political evolution from bronze to plastic.

A gust of cold air jerked him back to reality. It was night. The temperature had plummeted below zero. Too late to make the top now, too dark anyway. He must find sanctuary. Visions of Samantha materialized out of the swirling gloom.

His eleventh hour gazed back at him with gunmetal clarity, draining his strength, his will to go on. He would die there in that high place unless he found refuge. His hands and feet were numb as the frozen ice.

He heard Pasamenus calling his name. "Here, John, between these outcrops." He reached out his hand for his Marine Corps brother, fearful he might fall, clutching empty space. A cave! In he went, then banked up the snow around the entrance to seal in the warmth. Sergeant Kohn was there. Samantha Fox. Private Henry. Suzie Brown. Bubba Smith. His mother and father. His friend Pasamenus…

John opened his eyes to find Bubba shaking him. "Jesus Christ! You scared the shit outta me, man. You dreamin' again?"

Chapter Twenty

Okinawa

Okinawa is part of the Ryukyu Islands chain between Taiwan and Japan. It was the last major battleground of World War Two, before the American B-29 Enola Gay dropped the atomic bomb on Hiroshima. Okinawa varies in width from 2 to 17 miles and is 67 miles long. It was a major staging area in the Pacific for the Navy, the Marines, and the engines of war shipping out for Vietnam. The top secret SR-71 Blackbird was stationed there.

Concrete pillboxes and sunken Japanese freighters were still in evidence around the island in the 1960s. So was the Japanese airfield at Shuri Castle. Americans killed or reported missing numbered 12,520, following 83 bloody days of fighting, with more than 38,000 wounded. The Japanese were wiped out with 110,000 casualties. Thirty-six American ships had been sunk and 368 damaged. Sixteen ships were lost by the Japanese Navy, and 7,800 aircraft. A lot of brave men rested on the bottom of the East China Sea.

First Squad landed at midnight and were taken immediately to a mess hall where everyone onboard the flight was fed. After chow, the duty officer led them over to a Quonset hut complex where they were checked in and assigned a place to sleep. Next morning, they were up with the chickens for roll call, then back to the mess hall for breakfast. By midday, scuttlebutt had it they were shipping out for Japan the following weekend.

The officer of the day ordered his three rifle platoons to assemble out front of their Quonset huts at 1300 hours to read them a briefing from Headquarters in Da Nang. They were about to learn what fate held in store for them. The weather was a comfortable 68 degrees on their sunny island paradise. Bubba was the only member of First Squad with signs of battle damage, a half-moon black eye. The last they saw of Biker Boy, an ambulance crew was taking him away to the hospital.

"Listen up, men. Rather than read you the whole thing, I'm going to spell it out in plain English. Day after tomorrow at 0800 hours you will be leaving Okinawa for Da Nang. You are to have your gear assembled and ready at the flight terminal next door at 0720 hours. Chow is 0630 hours. You will be checked in and placed onboard your aircraft at 0740 hours. The rest of today and all of tomorrow you have to yourselves. I suggest you make the most of it, gentlemen. Where you're going is Indian Country. Good luck. Dismiss the troops, sergeant."

Most of the men headed over to the PX to buy swim trunks, then hightailed it for the beach. The sack rats went back inside to catch a few more Zs. The homesick brigade began writing letters home to mama and Betty Lou. First Squad elected to take a gander around the island.

They had wandered maybe two miles along a pristine shoreline when they came upon a concrete bunker with a gun port three feet high and thirteen feet across. A large caliber bomb or naval shell had blown open its 58-inch concrete and steel-reinforced roof. The rebar had blown downward from the blast and hung like stalactites inside a giant's abandoned helmet. Farther up the beach they discovered corroded .25 caliber cartridge casings scattered among the sea grass beneath a grove of palm trees, some with only half their trunks left standing. A thousand yards out to sea, the rusting hull of a ship poked her bow up above the green swells of the ocean. It was all so beautiful and serene. Private Henry thought it exotic and very romantic. Red thought so too. Only Pasamenus knew the history of the island, that twenty two years ago it had been a living inferno of hell and death. That information he kept to himself.

Chapter Twenty-One

Da Nang

Da Nang, like Saigon and Hue and so many other cities in Vietnam, was a beautiful, almost mythological place had it not been for the war. Da Nang was a favorite among the troops with its unique circle of low-lying mountains sitting out in the ocean, connected to the coastal plains by a narrow strip of beaches and military complexes, barely above sea level.

The headquarters of I Corps was located there. This was the key logistical center for the air and naval powers of the Northern Sector. Da Nang was a strategic coastal city, the fourth largest in Vietnam, situated only ninety-eight miles south of the Demilitarized Zone that separated North and South Vietnam.

Da Nang was one of the most exotic and interesting places along Vietnam's 2,025 miles of coastline. Mountains dropped straight down into the South China Sea, where they overlooked thirty kilometers of lush green palm trees and white sandy beaches. China Beach was there. Sixty-two miles west of the city began the country's border with Laos, then the Ho Chi Minh Trail. The Gulf of Tonkin was two hundred miles north where it eventually joined the port city of Haiphong. Twelve kilometers south of Da Nang lay the Marble Mountains. These consisted of five marble and limestone hills jutting up from a flat costal plain, each said to represent the five elements of the universe: water, wood, earth, metal, and fire.

The 17th Parallel cuts Vietnam in half. To the east, this imaginary line passes through Luzon and the Philippine Sea. West, it traverses Southern India. In the southern hemisphere, it cuts through the Yucatan Peninsula below Mexico City.

The coastline of Vietnam has two tropical monsoon seasons. Monsoon in the North takes place October through April with cloudy weather, constant fog, and frequent drizzle which may last for weeks at a time. Maximum rainfall comes between September and January. It gets cold during the winter months and sweltering hot in summer.

Monsoon in the South takes place May through September. During the remainder of the year, rainfall for the southern coastal region is light and often infrequent. Weather conditions in the South are somewhat more moderate than the North, although both sections of the country receive abundant rainfall during their monsoons seasons.

The beauty of the region was deceptive. The French had constructed an airbase there during the Occupation. The Marines landed at Da Nang in 1965 to make use of the old port facilities and those strategic concrete runways. But, by 1967, 200,000 peasants had migrated to the region, hoping for a few crumbs off the Yankee-Doodle supper table, which already had 100,000 peasants living there to begin with. By late November the place resembled a poor man's smorgasbord. Spies, deserters, prostitutes, drug peddlers, Vietcong, and a world of dirt poor Vietnamese, surrounding forty five square miles of American military complex.

The people of Vietnam are a marvelous breed of individuals.

Fun-loving, friendly, and 85% poor, they have weathered centuries of hardship and warfare throughout their many uprisings and battles against China for independence. France wrested control of the country away from the Vietnamese in the late 19th century, followed in 1940 by Imperial Japan. At the close of World War Two, France was back again, attempting to reestablish her old Colonial Rule, but this was finally laid to rest at the battle of Dien Bien Phu.

France and Vietnam signed the Geneva Peace Accords in the summer of 1954. But, because of pressures brought to bear by the Soviet Union and the People's Republic of China, Vietnam's delegates to the Geneva Conference agreed to a temporary partition of their nation at the 17th parallel to allow France a face-saving exit in the South. This face-saving maneuver was the result of the Korean War. China and Russia were nervous about ruffling the feathers of the American Eagle again so soon following Uncle Sam's 1953 armistice settlement at Panmunjom with North Korea.

The Geneva Accords partitioned the country at the Ben Hai River, with the unlikely promise of democratic elections to be held in 1956 to reunite the North with the South. But, rather than peaceful reunification, this well-intended partition led to the Vietnam War. Ho Chi Minh and the communists in Hanoi, and President Diem and his brother Nhu in Saigon were equally corrupt. And ruthless to the bone. Neither faction followed the mandates of the Peace Accords. This led to the wholesale abuse of the Vietnamese people, and thousands were murdered on both sides. Some labeled this a civil war. Civil or not, it evolved as the United States versus communist China and the USSR.

Master Sergeant Patrick Lucian Abernathy was a barrel-chested, self-contained, red-haired individual who had survived Guadalcanal, Bougainville, Iwo Jima, and the Chosen Reservoir. He didn't cotton much to officers, going by the book, or two-faced politicians, but he did love his Corps. His two great specialties in life were teaching young Marines how to stay alive, and inflicting maximum damage on the enemy. Forty-five years of age, never married, and an avid devotee of Italian opera, his favorite radio and television personality was Jimmy Durante. Patrick cursed like a professional and sometimes drank like one, but he did have a mama-san girlfriend living in town.

Spring of 1966, while on assignment in Da Nang, he came across a pretty Vietnamese lady sitting on the curb crying. "What have we here?" he asked. Being a gentleman of sorts he looked out for the weaker sex and Vietnamese youngsters.

Her slumlord had kicked her out for being unable to pay her rent. In lieu of rent, he asked the lady for sex. She refused, so out she went. They returned to her dilapidated two-room flat where Sergeant Abernathy paid her arrogant, tub-a-guts slumlord six months' rent in advance. He then busted the man's nose and cracked two ribs. Sun Li had no more problems following his departure.

"You people been assigned to me until a new batch a pilgrims arrive here the end a this here month. We're shorthanded, for whatever the dumb-ass SNAFU. You will then ship out for Hue for your next duty assignment. In the meantime, you will help guard the perimeter fence around this here base. This is an important assignment, people, so don't fall asleep and don't get your ass shot grab-assin'. Charlie is always out there, one or two clicks up in the hills. And he's always watching you. Our job is to make certain he don't get in here and fuck with Uncle Sam's aircraft. Now get down to Armory and draw your ammunition."

The 75 Marines of Platoon 43, freshly arrived from Parris Island, were divided into two separate rifle platoons, each one consisting of four fire teams, designated Platoon Four and Platoon Five. They would operate independently, but would remain together throughout their thirteen-month tour of duty. That night, before the men went on patrol, Gunny Abernathy spoke with them a second time.

"You see somethin' funny or strange on the ground, leave it the fuck alone. We got people makin' sweeps ever four hours looking for grenades an' crap like that. Stay in the shadows when they're available.

Don't stand in one spot too long. Charlie got eyes like a cat. You hear movement outside the fence, take cover then call it in. You see a hole cut in the fence, take cover then call it in. Something bothers you, find you some cover then get on the horn. Don't talk, whistle, or fart like a baboon. Remain silent at all times. Charlie don't shoot what he can't see or hear.

"We get mortar rounds comin' in about ever' week here lately. Don't worry about that. Sometimes they hit somethin'. Usually they land in a field someplace. We got choppers for that shit. The enemy is good with diversions. Little bastards will raise a ruckus one place, then shoot your ass off next door. So stay alert! Somethin' hits the ground, you hit the deck. It's a fuckin' grenade. You see enemy fire comin' your way, call in your position. Then explain his in detail. A chopper will be there in five minutes. If a firefight starts, it's normal to get scared. We all get twitchy when that happens. Just keep your heads down and remember to think. Thinkin' is what keeps your ass alive out here.

"A white man's face shines in the moonlight like a monkey's butt. Use burnt cork on your face and the back of your hands. You black fellows got it made. You got built-in camouflage. Tape them dog tags. Leave any loose change you got behind. Somethin' rattles, secure it or leave it. Make sure them shoelaces is tied tight. Never smoke on patrol. Once is all it takes to get your head blown off. Do not patrol back and forth in the same pattern. Lock and load once you reach the fence. If you see Charlie, use your thumb and forefinger to ease off the safety. He'll never hear you."

Fence patrol was easy. Damn near boring if there weren't folks out there trying to blow the place away. But the monsoon was a pain in the neck for both sides. No serious incidents took place worth writing home about. A few mortars did come in some nights but the Cobra gunships kept those down to a minimum. And the lousy weather. During the five weeks they spent at Da Nang, five enemy soldiers were shot and killed outside the perimeter fence. And one was taken prisoner. The boys were learning to use the night to their advantage.

Night before they shipped out for Hue, Gunny paid them a visit in the barracks. Patrick walked in with a quart of Old Grand-Dad in each hand. Gunny was a people person.

"Belly up, lads. It's time for a wee taste."

The men crowded around for the celebration. Johnson brought over a case of Coca-Cola they had stashed in a freezer chest while Pasamenus raided the maintenance locker for Dixie cups. Gunny poured each man a potent brew.

"Get comfortable. I wanna talk to you."

They pulled up locker boxes and buckets and empty ammo crates. Some sat on the bunks near the squad bay table. It was a jovial gathering between an old salt and his freshmen class of young warriors.

"You men are going to see some action soon. Some of it might get rough. We're in a fucking war. The politicians and lawyers stateside don't understand this shit. To them it's a big-ass chess game. But to you grunts out here in the field it's life and death. So remember this. Never take Charlie for granted. He's smart and he's good. Never give the bastard a break. If he's wounded and yellin' for help, stay clear. Chances are he ain't hurt. Probably got a grenade he's gonna roll on ya. A stranger runs up you don't know, shoot the son of a bitch. They got a hand grenade or a concealed weapon. These bastards use kids, old men, women, you name it. So always expect the unexpected."

"Top, what about booby traps? How can we spot those things?"

"That's a tough one, son. About all you can do is look for some kind of disturbance on the ground. Maybe the leaves are bent back or you see a broken limb or the earth has been disturbed. It's best to stay off the trails. And keep your eyes peeled for tripwires. You see prongs or a piece of metal sticking outta the ground, that's trouble. Mark it and move on."

The question-and-answer session lasted an hour. Finally, the whiskey was gone and everyone was in good spirits. It was time for Gunny to say good-bye.

"I saved the bad news for last, men. You pilgrims got a real live sumbitch for top sergeant once you reach Hue." He stopped talking and gazed away into space.

Finally, the men could stand it no longer. "Who, sir? Who is it, Gunny?"

"Yours by-god truly!" Patrick Lucian Abernathy smiled proudly. "My request for transfer came through two days ago. I'm leavin' with you fellas in the morning."

Chapter Twenty-Two

Suzie Brown

The Promise

January 1968: Initially, they began meeting for lunch on Mondays when Suzie had her day off. But as the days progressed into weeks, their rendezvous changed to Friday night dinners at Pero's Greek Restaurant on Kingston Pike in West Knoxville. Samantha enjoyed the drive from Alcoa, and their evenings together sharing girl talk. From the restaurant, she drove out Chapman Highway to Colonial Village to spend her weekends with Miss Martha.

The food was good and the prices reasonable, especially Pero's scrumptious spaghetti. And the wine list presented an adequate variety of selections. Pero's was a nice family restaurant with a Mediterranean atmosphere, so the two beautiful women didn't have to fend off the male set very often, although the waiters were taken with them both.

"I don't watch the news anymore. All they talk about is something depressing. How many deaths occurred this week in the war. Whose child was run over by a school bus. They don't seem to care how it affects people who listen to their gloom and doom. Especially if you have a family member over there."

"I know it. I take the newspaper but all I read are the comics and the fashion section. The front page is all about politics and Vietnam. I worry more if I read that stuff."

"Have you seen The Graduate?"

"No, have you?"

"No. There's another one I want to see too. In The Heat Of The Night with Rod Steiger and Sidney Poitier."

"We oughta go one night next week."

"I'll bring Martha. She loves the movies."

"Good idea. We could have dinner, then go."

"Have you heard from Robert?"

"I got a letter this week. He said they're someplace called Da Nang. That's a funny name. He said it was safe there. All they do is train and work on equipment. And it's very pretty. And close to the ocean. I wonder if it really is safe?"

"John wrote that too. He said there's a place there called Monkey Mountain. It sounds nice. I hope it's not dangerous. Some nights I can't sleep for worrying. I've lost six pounds since John left."

"You aren't eating your spaghetti, either."

"All right, smarty-pants. I'll eat my sketti if it makes you happy."

They laughed and proceeded with the meal.

"Are you very busy at the salon?

"Swamped! I'd like to open up my own place one of these days. How 'bout you?"

"Oh, I stay busy. But my heart isn't in it anymore. I miss John so much it's messing up my menstrual cycles. Maybe I should try sleeping tablets."

"Sugarplum, I know what you need!"

"Ooooh! You're awful. Well, that too. I'm just afraid, you know, he might not come home."

"I pray a lot, Sam. I ask God that if one of us has to die, let it be me. You can come stay at my place anytime you're feeling down. I have an extra bedroom. We can drink wine, go to church, watch the movies, whatever it takes to get us through this."

"I wish I was strong like you. I am with my job, but when it comes to John I'm just a big baby. I miss him so much."

"Bubba's a dreamboat. Up until he asked me to marry him I was empty as old Mother Hubbard's cupboard. I have to believe God will bring them back to us. My faith is what keeps me going. Don't let fear take control of your life."

"I know. Maybe if I started going to church more often. There's a cute little church over where Martha lives. I'll ask her to go Sunday."

"I go to Graystone Presbyterian. You guys can come go with me anytime."

"I'd like that. So would Martha. She just turned fifty. Her health is good but she's the other person I worry about. She's such a sweet lady. I wish I could find someone special for her. I'm gone most of the time and she's there by herself."

"We'll find her a millionaire. Then they can look after us poor puds." The women laughed and sipped their wine.

'Now about that movie. Which one would you like to see?"

"Oh, The Graduate I guess."

"That's downtown. We could go to Regas Restaurant for dinner."

"John and I went there once. We liked it."

"Come in the shop next week and I'll fix your hair. Nothing like a little primping to make a girl feel better."

"You're right about that other thing. I miss making love with John. When you love someone, it's so wonderful. You give him everything, your mind, your heart, your body. I miss waking up with him beside me, reaching over…having breakfast afterward."

"Don't even talk about it, you naughty girl. I'll have to go home and get my vibrator."

Samantha cackled. "You're so funny. You cheered me up tonight. I'm glad we're friends. Bubba's lucky to have you."

"Don't I know it." They laughed again. "Want to go to the VFW for a drink before we head home."

"Sure." They split the tab, left a generous tip, then headed for the nightspot in Suzie's red Mustang.

The bar was two deep with noisy patrons celebrating Thank God It's Friday. The atmosphere was friendly and folks were having a good time. A lady stopped by their table, asking Suzie where she got her hair done. Suzie handed the woman a business card and told her to call next Tuesday for an appointment.

"This place sure is busy."

"Yeah, I come here once in a while to break the monotony of being by myself all the time."

"And all these men. Do they, like, come on to you?"

"Honey, like ducks after a June bug. But I'm saving that special treat for Mister Bubba."

"They do me too. In the White Stores, everyplace I go."

"That's just the way men are."

"Do you think John and Bubba are ever tempted?"

"Maybe…but Bubba made me a promise. He said he would never be with another woman. I didn't ask, he just up and said it before he left."

"I trust my Johnny too. Before he joined the Marines, he was in trouble all the time. Now it's like he's found peace, writing me how much he loves me and thinks about me. We're two of the lucky ones, aren't we, Suzie?"

"Yes, Sam. We certainly are."

Two men approached their table, asking them to dance. They explained they were married and were just there for cocktails. The men departed. It happened again before they decided to leave and go someplace else. Samantha suggested The Paris Café. Once inside, they were escorted to a couch in the back room beside the piano. The piano player was off sick with a sore throat.

"John and I came here quite a bit before we got married."

"I love this place. We come here once a week from the shop."

"This is fun. We should do this more often. It helps my head."

"Some women would kill to have a head like yours. So many of them want to look pretty. I do my best, but some ladies just aren't, well, very attractive. You, on the other hand, are beautiful even without your makeup on."

"Why thank you, ma'am…please don't stop."

"There you go, talking about sex again." They howled with laughter.

"How did you meet John?"

"We met at Bill's Barn one night when I dropped by for a drink with a girlfriend. He was sitting in a booth with Robert. I noticed him first thing. Then he looked over at me and those colored lights began to flicker. I think I fell in love with John that first night. What about you? When did you know Bubba was the one?"

"Well, that's a long story. I knew Bubba, John too, from high school."

"I know…I mean…"

"You know?"

"Yes, well. OK, I have a confession to make. A friend, a so-called male friend, tried to break up John and I by telling me about his wild past, all about him and Robert. He talked about you some too."

"About me?"

"He said you were wild, like them. So I didn't like you because of your relationship with John and Robert. I guess it was jealousy more than anything else. But our going away party that night at Walnut Ridge. That was all your idea. I saw then, that night, and ever since then, what a big heart you have. What I'm trying to say so poorly…what happened years ago is none of my business. It doesn't matter anymore."

Tears leaked from Suzie's blue eyes and ran down her cheeks. She dabbed at her face with her handkerchief, sniffling. "You don't hate me?"

"I could never hate you, sweetie. I think we're best friends."

"I never thought I'd say this, but I'm glad you know. Your friendship means a lot to me, Samantha. So many times I was afraid somebody might tell you. I was such a wild thing when I was young, all screwed up and crazy. I feel like a big weight has been lifted off me."

"Don't let the boys know. This secret is between us, OK?"

"Sure. I guess we are best friends, aren't we? I never knew anybody like you before. I grew up poor as a church mouse. People like you and Bubba and John were so distant from me back then. I never thought I'd be in a place like this or friends with you guys."

"Well here we are, and we certainly are friends. I propose a toast. To friendship, Suzie and Sam. May we promise always to be there for one another and to remain best friends, come what may."

The women clinked glasses and repeated the words. Then they laughed and hugged one another. A burden had been lifted off Suzie. And Samantha had found a friend to confide in whenever the world flew off its axis.

The following Friday afternoon, Sam and Miss Martha met Suzie downtown in the Regas lounge for dinner. Afterward, they went to see The Graduate at the Tennessee Theatre. Coming back outside on the sidewalk, Miss Martha was taken with the ending of the picture show.

"Wasn't that something, him jamming that cross in the church doors? That was just perfect. Like the cross was protecting the love between that girl and boy against the people inside. Wasn't it romantic?"

"It sure was. Then they jumped on the bus with her wearing her wedding gown. I love happy endings."

"Why didn't you ever marry?" Samantha was suddenly struck by the notion. She had never asked Martha before.

"There was a young man once. We met in Sandy Springs at a lumber company of all places. I went there to buy some nails for a loose board on my house. He worked in the office. He was an average-looking man, but very nice. I liked him right away. His name was Fletcher Magbee."

"Did he take you out?"

"Oh, yes. That was 1941. The Depression was still with us then. There was trouble in Europe with Hitler. We dated, went dancing. Oh, I had a crush on Fletcher, all right."

"Well, what happened?"

"We both were shy. I remember the first time he kissed me. I think it embarrassed him. So I kissed him back." Miss Martha placed her hands over her heart, recalling her special moments during the war years when she was a young woman in love.

"Oh, you didn't. That's precious."

"Yes, I did! Then the Japanese bombed Pearl Harbor. Fletcher asked me out that Friday. At dinner that night he told me he had joined the Navy. He asked me to wait for him and I promised I would. We made love our first time. I stayed with Fletcher that whole wonderful weekend. Monday morning he left for the service."

"He wasn't serious?"

"Oh, Martha…"

"You darling things. He wasn't like that. He was a good man. We wrote love letters back and forth. Fletcher was killed in a sea battle near an island called Rabaul. I never stopped waiting, really. I just never fell in love again."

The fears inside the two young women came bubbling to the surface. Samantha broke down in tears. Then Suzie began to cry. Martha shooed them back to the car and drove them both to her place. That weekend she would take care of the two of them rather than the other way around. Later that night, after she had them tucked in bed, she drove out Chapman Highway to the bootlegger and purchased a fifth of vodka.

Sunday morning they attended Lake Forest Presbyterian. After church, she fixed Southern fried chicken, potato salad, green beans, and Bloody Marys. A sizable number of Bloody Marys. Samantha now had two confidantes. And Miss Martha had acquired herself a second daughter.

Chapter Twenty-Three

Hue

God unzipped the sky and whizzed on their parade. The monsoon season was in full swing when they flew into Hue in the midst a torrential downpour. Rain and fog so thick the men could barely see which way to run for the air terminal. From inside the airplane it resembled a gray ghost with a faintly visible beacon on top for a derby. Out they went, splashing across the tarmac and into the arms of history. Their average age was twenty-two. They were about to face the greatest challenge of their lives.

Hue was the imperial capital of Vietnam from 1802 until 1945. The Empire of Japan capitulated in August, formally surrendering September 2, 1945, onboard the USS Battleship Missouri. That same day, the North Vietnamese communists declared Hanoi to be their city of independence. This triggered the First Indochina War with France which lasted from November 20, 1946, until the French were defeated at the battle of Dien Bien Phu between March and May of 1954.

The city was of great historical significance, being the former cultural and religious center for a once-united Vietnam. But Hue was difficult to defend because of its vulnerable location so close to the Demilitarized Zone, the A Shau Valley, and the Ho Chi Minh Trail. The A Shau Valley lay just twenty-five miles northwest.

Hue was part of I Corps, and the northernmost command center for ground forces in Vietnam. Other important northern cities used by I Corps were Chu Lai and Quang Tri. First and Third Marine Divisions were stationed around Hue and Da Nang, strung out below the DMZ and southwest alongside the Laotian border. The ARVN 1st Infantry Division was billeted inside Hue's ancient Citadel. US Army forces were stationed in force outside the city and throughout the northern jungles. Australian forces were there as well, their numbers peaking in Vietnam at more than 7,000 in 1969.

The South Korean military appeared in 1965 in the form of a few officers and a medical unit. They quickly expanded and fielded a brigade that grew. Between 1965 and 1973, 312,000 South Korean soldiers served in Vietnam. The Philippines sent 10,450 troops. These men and women represented quality personnel.

Additional troops would soon be arriving in Hue on orders from General Westmoreland. The British and the French never participated in the Vietnam War. Their governments hung back, siding with the liberal news media and the antiwar Left. Thailand, New Zealand, and the Republic of China (Taiwan) also deployed small contingents during the war.

During the ten-year involvement of the American Armed Forces, 320,000 Chinese soldiers and 3,000 Russians served in North Vietnam. Primarily, these were construction workers, technicians, doctors and nurses, and military personnel.

Several American military units were stationed with I Corps during the fighting: 82nd Airborne Division; 9th Marine Amphibious Brigade; Fifth Infantry Division; First Cavalry Division (Airmobile);

Third Marine Division; First Marine Division; First Brigade; 101st Airborne Division; American Division; XXIV Corps; III Marine Amphibious Force.

Gunny's company was billeted in the French barracks outside the city. Built during the Occupation, they were old and somewhat run-down but comfortable. And much appreciated over the canvas tents where many of the Army personnel were quartered.

"Y'all see that new Playboy? Connie Kreski looks kinda like Sam. Sam's prettier, though. More armor plate up-front too, if you know what I mean."

"Careful, ole son. You'll be givin' away family secrets." Bubba grinned, envisioning his own sexy Suzie in the buff.

"I liked Miss March last year. She got hooters, man! I get twitchy just thinkin' 'bout them big, purty Tootsie Pops." Red was a breast connoisseur.

"I always liked women with big breasts!" John loved Sam's 36 inch C-cup twins. The rest of her was pretty amazing too.

"When I get back, I'm getting me one a them 38 D women."

"Red, short as you are they'll be hangin' over your shoulders when y'all dance."

The squad heehawed. Red continued. "They can hang out the window just so's I get me one. Hell, I may get two! Monday, Wednesday, and Friday for number Uno. Tuesday, Thursday, and Saturday for my Ducey baby doll. Sundays, I take off an' go fishin'."

"Sounds like a plan, ole son." Bubba was quite fond of his cousin Red. "You get'cha a purty woman, me an' John'll get our ole ladies, and we'll all go out dancing, Walnut Ridge maybe."

"That would be killer, hoss. We'll do 'er when we get back."

"If you're going to assemble all those pretty ladies for a social event, perhaps I will pay Knoxville a visit and find a suitable lady for myself." Armenian curiosity had been aroused.

"Brain, you come down where I live. I'll fix you up with a sho'nuff coon-ass!" Johnson held brotherly affection for his intellectual friend. "Ain't nothin' better than a Cajun woman. Them gals'll steam up yer glasses, turn ya ever' which way but loose, then cook up a mess uh gumbo an' collard greens with red beans an rice. Oooweee!"

John responded. "By golly, we'll all come down! What a party that would be!"

"Yeah, we oughta do that. Go down maybe when they got Mardi Gras."

"We'll drink loud mouth an' get sideways drunk!"

"What is this loud mouth?"

"Drinkin' liquor…the more you drink the louder you get!"

"Yes, indeed. I shall look forward to getting halfways with you fellows."

"It's sideways, Brain. Not halfways."

"Then I will become sideways drinking loud mouth with the big-breasted hooter lady."

They all laughed and slapped him on the shoulders. Not only was Brain the smartest member of the group, he was something of a mascot for them. They teased him about his proper English, but each man respected Pasamenus as one shows deference to an elder sibling.

"It's two hours 'til lights out. Let's hit the slop-shoot for a beer."

Down at the enlisted man's bar and recreation center they ordered their Pabst Blue Ribbons, then crowded around a table beside another table of enlisted Air Force personnel. The conversation continued on for another hour about women and home. Big-breasted women! Then Pasamenus placed a finger to his lips, nodding toward the table next door.

"I was standing right there while he was talking with his wingman."

"That don't make no sense."

"Well, he said it."

"You mean we can't hit them sites 'til they're hot"

"I was right there, man, inspecting the pilot's nosegear."

"Because of the Chinks and the Russians?"

"That's not all. We can't hit the compounds where they live, neither."

"God, I hate this war!"

Back at the barracks, Pasamenus explained to the squad what he had overheard before he signaled for quiet to hear the remainder of a troubling conversation.

"Our pilots are not allowed to attack the surface-to-air missile batteries until they are completed and fully operational."

"But why?"

"Because Russian and Chinese technicians are building them."

"Big deal. So what?"

"It seems Washington doesn't want to antagonize the Soviets or the Chinese by our pilots killing their technicians."

"That's fucking crazy!"

"Yes, it appears we are restricted in strange ways."

"Sweet Jesus! That explains us havin' them dumb-ass firebases all over the place, like forts in the Old West. That's another load a by-god crazy. Why ain't we trackin' down them commie rat bastards up North, hoss?"

"I'm afraid that is a question only the politicians can answer, Red."

"Remember that old general back at Parris Island? He said the same thing that day we graduated. He said we needed new leaders."

"Yes, Henry, I was putting it all together back at the canteen. It looks as though we're fighting this war with one arm tied behind our backs."

Driggins posed a question to Pasamenus. "Wasn't Korea like this?"

"President Truman forbade our fighter pilots from pursuing the Russian MiGs back to their fighter bases in China. We never bombed those MiG-15 bases. Nor any of the Chinese border towns where China assembled her troops. And we never bombed their bridges over the Yalu River. General MacArthur wanted to expand the war into China, but he was fired by President Truman. Yes, Vietnam does appear to be as dysfunctional as the Korean War."

That night the men turned in with feelings of uncertainty and frustration. For the remainder of the month everything went by the book. Guard duty, letters home, barracks repair, chow, latrine duty, junk-on-the-bunk inspections, more guard duty. Then, one night, Gunny assembled Fourth Platoon in the squad bay upstairs.

Chapter Twenty-Four

The Valley of the Shadow

The A Shau Valley had a mystique about it, an aura of intrigue and mystery, and of evil lurking back among the trees. The Montagnard tribesmen living there called the place The Valley of the Shadow of Death. For centuries, invading armies from the north had fought and died along its thirty-five miles of trails, jungle, and inland waterways.

Mountains ran the length of the valley on both sides, ranging in elevations from 1,000 up to 6,800 feet. The valley floor varied in width from a single kilometer across to as many as four or five kilometers. Part of the jungle was double and triple canopy. There were tigers and elephants, monkeys, parrots, wild pigs, open plains, elephant grass, and bamboo as big around as a man's leg. The Rao Lao (A Sap) River ran through the valley, parallel with Route 548 for a few kilometers, then it meandered away. Route 548 was a serviceable dirt road with wooden bridges constructed by the Vietnamese during the French Colonial Period. It was one of several dirt roads in the valley.

The valley was notorious for foul weather, especially heavy fog, giving helicopter and bomber pilots fits. This served as protective cover for the NVA and Vietcong. A Special Forces camp was overrun in the northern sector of the valley in March of 1966, partly because of overcast skies and rain. But it wasn't until the spring of 1968, when American and ARVN forces returned in strength that the fighting began in earnest. The north end of the valley was only three and a half miles from the Laotian border, then began the Ho Chi Minh Trail. The Trail ran the length of Vietnam just beyond the borders of Laos and Cambodia. Hue lay just twenty-five miles east from the south end of the Valley.

The bones of thousands of invaders lay buried beneath its fertile soil before the North Vietnamese Army and their Vietcong guerrillas clashed with South Vietnam, which was backed by the United States and her Allies. In the northern end of the A Shau was a communist stronghold designated as Base Area 611, ringed with a formidable array of antiaircraft batteries. Dozens of American aircraft were lost there during the war.

Operation Apache Snow took place in the A Shau Valley, just south of Base Area 611. As part of this operation, an assault on Hill 937 began May 10, 1969. This assault was termed "Hamburger Hill" by elements of the press. Assigned to this effort were three infantry battalions from the 101st Airborne Division: The 3rd Battalion, 187th Infantry, 2nd Battalion, 501st Infantry, and the 1st Battalion, 506th Infantry. Two battalions from the ARVN 1st Division also participated in the assault. Two additional battalions from the ARVN 1st Division were engaged in another sector of the battle, including three battalions from the 9th Marine Regiment, plus the 3rd/5th Calvary Regiment.

Like Khe Sahn, this battle, which lasted ten bloody days, was questioned by the media and members of Congress. Seventy Americans were killed and 372 wounded. ARVN casualties also ran high, with an estimated 700 North Vietnamese soldiers killed. But the Ap Bia Mountain and her sister elevations were of no strategic importance to the Allies. After the battle was finally won, this hard-fought-for real estate was quietly abandoned on June 5th. Public outrage followed. General Abrams, on orders from President Nixon, then switched from a policy of "maximum pressure" to one of "protective reaction." The Tet Offensive in 1968 was the turning point in the Vietnam War. Apache Snow and the battle of Hamburger Hill in 1969 was the last military straw.

December 1967: "Men, we got ourselves a mission in the A Shau Valley, Charlie Country. We're going in with one platoon, you people, to reconnoiter an area on the south end where Intelligence says they's a commie supply dump. Fly boys can't find the sumbitch so we're it. Drop your cocks and grab your socks 0500. The choppers will pick us up after chow. You'll need your ponchos, poncho liners, shelter halves, extra socks, skivvies, and toiletries. Clean your rifles before you hit the sack. Everything else we need will be onboard the choppers tomorrow morning. We may be out there a few days so bring soap, and don't forget your foot powder and bug juice. Fall Out!"

"It's almost Christmas and we're going out in the boondocks!"

"Give it a rest, Jarhead. What else we got to do around here?"

"Stay warm for one thing…and have a dry place to sleep."

"Fresh air will do us good." Bubba fancied himself the outdoorsman.

"Snakes and skeeters…get chomped by a damn leopard, maybe." John fancied his comforts.

"Not leopards, John. They're tigers. Asian tigers." Pasamenus, ever the informed one.

"I seen one a them wampus cats last week. Varmit looked plumb hungry, like." Red, the comic. Cousin Bubba snickered.

"He had a mess kit with 'im. Looked like he was fixin' to chomp his bad self a white boy." More laughter at Johnson's ribbing Private Jackson.

"He was over at the PX a month ago buyin' salt-and-pepper shakers. Sho'nuff!"

Driggins piped in. "I hear they like Southern white meat best, with squashed taters an' gravy on it."

"You guys'll sing a different tune if one a them things shows up. I saw one in the Atlanta Zoo. They're big as Johnson's an' Bubba's fat asses put together."

"Knock it off over there! We gotta get up early."

The ride from Hue to the A Shau Valley lasted half an hour. Then the choppers lifted away, leaving thirty-eight men standing waist deep in morning fog. Ponchos and flack jackets were the order of the day.

A chill was on the valley floor, accompanied by light rain. The Marine baby-sans were losing their cherries. Gunny pulled out a map, studied the terrain, then pointed northeast.

"Up there someplace. Stay off the road. We'll follow this creekbed."

Four miles farther along the waterway, they arrived at a sizable pond full of colorful waterbirds and lilies with purple blossoms. John recognized the blue-and-white herons as similar to ones he and Sam had seen on a picnic in Louisville Park. But instead of proceeding farther up the road, Gunny led them around behind the marsh and into the trees. Sparse vegetation quickly became fronds with hanging vines everywhere. Trees rose up fifty feet, becoming ever denser as they proceeded away from the central plain and into the jungle.

It was Pasamenus who found the cave in a wall of rock rising straight up at the base of a steep hill resting against the eastern mountain range. The entrance was about five feet high and wide enough for a man to slip through. Inside they discovered a large chamber, more than enough room to hold a platoon. Gunny marked it on the map and they moved on.

Arc Light B-52 bombing at the far end of the valley went off on schedule. Even twenty miles away it sounded like the end of the world. Rolling thunder, as hundreds of 500- and 750-pound bombs rained down from 35,000 feet on Base Area 611. The horizon lit up through the rain clouds and drizzle.

They proceeded to the top of the hill where it leveled out in a half-moon plateau. Mountains directly behind them rose up 3,000 feet. From there they could see for several miles in both directions. Gunny spread them out in a perimeter defense, then out came the C rations. Still no signs of an ammo dump.

"Look up there. What is that?"

A glow had appeared in the clouds, coming their way.

"What the hell is that?"

"Check your weapons, lads!"

It broke through the cloud cover three miles up the valley. The fighter was streaming a plume of fire and smoke behind its damaged engine. It had been struck by an air-to-air missile, and the pilot was attempting to land and save the aircraft.

They watched in awe as the engine flamed out and quit. The jet fighter fell from a hundred feet, full flaps, striking the ground hard a mile north of them in the center of the valley. The jet bounced high in the air, angling back down nose-first, shearing off a section of the right wing as tons of steel and aluminum came skidding through the underbrush, coming to rest just north of their position.

"Red Star! That's a MiG! First Squad! Get your asses down there and capture that joker. The rest of you monkeys check your magazines. We'll be gettin' visitors soon."

The MiG-21 had broken in half behind the swept wing assembly, the tail section coming to rest sideways beside the cockpit. The right wing was on fire. The whole aircraft was in danger of going up in flames and taking the pilot with it. They found him pounding on the canopy, but the canopy was jammed.

Pasamenus pulled out his trench knife and began prying at the apparatus. Johnson and Bubba went to work with their bayonets. John and the others spread out in defensive positions. It wasn't working. They could see the fear in the pilot's face.

"Try this." Pasamenus attached his bayonet to his M-14 and began prying at the metal collar around the base of the clear Plexiglass.

Bubba followed suit. Johnson used the butt of his rifle to try and break the glass. His metal butt plate broke loose. The flames were inching along the broken wing, licking up on their side of the fuselage. The trapped pilot was in a crouched position, pushing against the canopy with his back.

"Stand clear." Pasamenus fired a round into the leading edge of the metal collar. Then a second round. A third round. It moved an inch. He fired again. Johnson began swinging his rifle until the stock broke. Bubba was prying hard with his bayonet. His bayonet broke. The canopy slid two more inches.

"Stand clear." Pasamenus empted eleven rounds, full automatic, into the front edge of the collar. The fire was all underneath the wing now. Still no go. Johnson climbed up on the nose of the aircraft, kicking at the canopy, again, again, again. It moved. The last time he kicked the canopy, it slid a foot and he fell off the airplane with Bubba breaking his fall. The pilot squeezed out, falling to the ground, exhausted.

"Come on! Let's go!"

They were a hundred feet away when 850 liters of aviation fuel exploded in an orange fireball, then 30 mm cannon shells began whizzing around them.

"Run!" The pilot needed no translation for that.

He spoke English with a thick accent. "Thank you for saving my life." Pasamenus spoke to him in his native Armenian language. The pilot answered Pasamenus in Russian.

When they were back on top of the plateau, Pasamenus introduced Gunny to Demetri. Up the valley a little over a mile they saw an army of VC pouring out of the trees on their right. A couple of hundred it seemed, more were farther up the valley. Thousands more. It was time to saddle up and hit the trail.

"All right, you. Any funny business and I'll put a bullet in your head. Understand?"

"I will not betray you, sergeant. Your men saved my life. I am your grateful prisoner."

"See to it you stay that way. Lads, follow me!"

Gunny led them down the hill to the cave. Once his men and the Russian were inside, he went back to the base of the hill, arranging the weeds and bushes so everything looked as natural as possible. Then he dusted the ground behind him with a small bush while retracing his steps to the cave.

"This is Red Dog. Do you copy?" Nothing but static. "This is Red Dog. Red Dog. Come in, jokers. Do you copy?"

More static. They were not receiving him. He was too close to the mountain, iron ore in the rocks, something. Gunny gave Pasamenus his instructions, then stuffed his duster inside the cave opening and set out west toward the river.

Half a mile from the cave he tried a third time. It worked. Beyond the perimeter of the trees he heard them talking and laughing, searching for their lost pilot. He radioed his coordinates, calling down an air strike on his position. He called for a second strike two kilometers due north.

Gunny lay still for nearly an hour, concealed beneath the bushes with his pals the mosquitoes and a couple of pesky leeches. The North Vietnamese had moved in all around him still searching for their pilot, so he was forced to remain silent. His little friends got their bellies full.

The first string of bombs blew the limbs off the trees in front of his position. Screams rang out from mortally wounded men. This was it. Up he rose from his hiding place. Two Vietcong standing right beside him began fumbling with their weapons and yelling. Gunny cut them down with his Thompson submachine gun, then ran for the cave. Bomb blasts began erupting everywhere. Shrapnel and debris filled the air. It was going to be virgin-pussy tight. A few more yards and he spotted the rocky face of the hill.

"Come on, old man. You can do this!"

With the Grim Reaper chasing after his behind, he ran for all he was worth…tripped over a vine…hit the ground rolling and came up running, clutching the Thompson out front. Concussion from a bomb blast hurled him sideways into a grove of bamboo. Dazed and bleeding from his nose and ears, he staggered back on his feet…helmet lost, he labored on, lungs sucking for oxygen. Gunny clawed his way through the cave opening as the forest behind him was swept away by napalm and high explosives.

The men inside rushed around their sergeant lying on the ground, placing a pack under his head for support. One of the new boys gave him water from his canteen. Bubba touched the leech on his neck with the glowing tip of a cigarette. The thing squirmed off and was squashed. They all began talking at once.

Gunny held up his hand for quiet, still catching his breath. "Just listen…a minute."

They fell silent and listened while the bombardment rolled up the right side of the valley. Suddenly the floor of the cave quaked, followed by a gigantic explosion. Tons of munitions, machine guns, mortars, antiaircraft weapons, mines, the whole nine yards were erupting in flaming mushrooms of arms and ammunition.

"That's the dump we was sent here to find. Charlie comin' outta the boonies gave it away. Remember that, Marines. You go out lookin' for somethin' and see a herd a those jokers, that's usually where it's at."

Demetri lit one, then handed the Soviet-Bloc cigarette to Gunny. "I wish my people's army was like this. Your men respect you. They care about you. In my army, the men are often mistreated by those with rank. Very sad for them. I think I don't wish to go back there again."

Henry emerged from the shadows of the cave with a smile on his face. "Guys, it's Christmas Eve!"

The drizzle had finally stopped leaving a damp chill in the night air. The jungle was cold and wet, surreal and ghostly in appearance. Stars speckled the evening sky, making their first encore in more than a week. The valley floor glowed with the pale illumination of a crescent moon, covered by a blanket of fog rising from the creek bottoms and the banks of the river. The fog moved and shifted on a gentle night wind.

Three sentries posted on top of the plateau gazed out across their imagined inland sea, while up the valley glowed the shattered remains of the ammunition dump. Shadows lay on the silent elevations where the children of the Apocalypse watched and waited. A Jurassic world for the encampment of the damned, where strange waters coupled with treacherous shores for aberrant journeymen.

Mountains across the valley floor lay hidden beneath miles of rain clouds, embracing dark peaks where legions once dwelled, leaching the bones of centuries past. Downwind, a mountain tiger gave vent to the exhilaration of the kill. Elephants grazing on the plain below paid her no mind in the gathering mists. The A Sap River swirled and eddied this night in the land of giants and dangerous men.

"This place gives me the creeps."

"You think their souls are set free if they're killed here before their time?"

"Wha'da ya mean?"

"Like, maybe, they become trapped here in the valley?"

"You mean ghosts?"

"More like spirits, stayin' here 'til Judgment Day."

"If that's the case, they're purty full up. The Brain says they been fightin' in here ever since forever."

"Think about it. All those people killed today and here we are, watchin' herd over our own guys sleepin' in a friggin' cave. Thousands of miles from the Southern Circle. Sittin' up here like the Lone Ranger with starlight scopes on these big-ass rifles in a valley fulla dead men. Things like this happen ever' thousand years, maybe."

"It is weird."

"Henry says when you kill a man you take the place of God."

"That boy ain't right. He'll pray over Charlie once he shoots one."

"Probably. But it makes you think, don't it?"

Red spoke for the first time. "I'd rather be God than be a dead sumbitch."

"I wonder if the stuff that happens in here is kept in some kinda record?"

"You havin' them dreams again?" John's nightmares concerned Robert.

"No. Just wonderin'."

"We're goin' home, OK? Someday we'll look back on this looney-tune place and tell big fat whoppers to our spoiled-ass grandkids."

"It sure is beautiful country, though." Red was comparing the A Shau Valley with the Smoky Mountains of East Tennessee.

"It sure is. You reckon many people are buried around here?"

"Thousands, maybe. I don't much care so's I ain't one of 'em."

"They can have this place. The whole country's nuts, people killin' each other over politics and religion. An' we're slap in the middle of it."

"I wish I knew things better, like Pasamenus. He called Vietnam a Garden of Eden. Then he said the real one was in Iraq."

"Wonder if Eve had 38 Ds? That would be something, hangin' out with your baby doll all day in the Garden, just lettin' it all hang out."

"No, Red. She had curly red hair, just like you, and she was flat-chested to boot."

"Dang! And I was all set to stay here if she popped outta the shrubbery."

"Then Adam shows up an whups your butt. Ours too for bein' associated with a deviant influence."

"Guess I better stick with them baby dolls over in Vestal and Virginia Heights!"

"Right on, brother!"

"Some dude in the mess hall called this place a clubfooted clusterfuck. Vietnam may look like the Garden of Eden, but it's nothing but a damn tar baby. I'll take the hills of Tennessee any day over this lash-up. At least back there we won't get shot by some commie rat bastard goin' to the Circle."

"Wonder what they're doin' at the Circle tonight? I miss that place, don't you?"

"Yeah, I sure do. We had fun, didn't we? All them crazy nights. I hope we get back OK. I'd hate to go home to Suzie with my eyes fucked up or my legs still over here in this hellhole."

"We'll get back. Johnson says Sarge is charmed. He gets hurt but they can't kill 'im. He ran through them bombs today and all he got was scratches. Long as we stick with Gunny, we'll be OK."

"Johnson's pretty cool. Sarge does seem to have nine lives."

"Guys…look."

Down below the fog had parted. The Vietcong were retrieving their dead. They sat and watched the grim proceedings until the fog closed in again. An hour later they were relieved.

When they got back to the cave, they were surprised to find Gunny and the Russian sitting around a small fire drinking C ration cocoa. Pasamenus and Johnson were with them. It was a few minutes after midnight, Christmas Day 1967.

Demetri was relating his experiences as a little boy at Stalingrad when the city was under siege by the German Sixth Army. They listened while he told his tale of the terrible cold, and nothing to eat, and frozen dead men everywhere. His mother peeled the wallpaper off the walls, scraped off the dried glue, then made them soup with warm water. She boiled a pair of leather shoes. They tried eating those but none of them could get the pieces down. One day she found Irish potatoes in the rucksack of a dead German soldier. A great feast followed.

The Russian pilot recalled fondly his mother and his three older sisters. One evening, while he was away scavenging for something to bring them to eat, a German phosphorus bomb struck their home. The house burned to the ground. There was nothing left of his family. Afterward, he nearly starved to death. Finally, the Russian soldiers took him in and gave him what little they could spare. He slept in the ruins with the soldiers. They taught him how to use a bolt-action Mauser rifle. Demetri killed his first man when he was seven years old. After the war, when he was old enough, he joined the Soviet Air Force.

Pasamenus told about his mother's and father's experiences at the hands of the Nazis. Late in the war, his father and four other partisans mined the railroad tracks near their hometown. When the troop train came through on its way to the Eastern Front, they exploded the tracks and many of the German soldiers were injured or killed. Two days later, the SS arrived. His mother and father hid in the belltower and watched. All the townspeople were rounded up and herded into the schoolhouse beside the village square. The doors and windows were boarded up and nailed shut. Then the SS men set fire to the building. Nearly three hundred people burned to death.

Sergeant Abernathy shared a few of his wartime experiences. Guadalcanal, and the night one lone machine gunner was all that stood between the Japanese and Henderson Field. Patrick received his first silver star on Guadalcanal. Iwo Jima, where five Marines and a Navy Corpsman raised the Stars and Stripes on Mount Suribachi. The underground Jap bunkers, and his buddies being shot to pieces. And the sad story of Ira Hayes, the whiskey-drinking Pima Indian.

They talked into the night while the Caucasian boys from Knoxville and their Negro friend from Magnolia Springs sat and listened to a Russian, an Armenian, and a Marine Corps Master Sergeant relate their stories of war and survival. That night, in the belly of a mountain in a millennial backwater of gathering violence, far from the land of Mickey Mouse and Uncle Remus, they bore witness to two generations of politics and warfare. It made a lasting impression on the men from Tennessee. Marcus Johnson and his mother were already familiar with segregation, but not to the extent the Russian people suffered under the Third Reich. Before they turned in, Gunny pulled out a flask from his pack. Everybody took a nip of Jack Daniels.

"Merry Christmas, lads.

"Merry Christmas, Gunny. You too, Demetri."

The Russian handed out the last of his tart cigarettes. "Happy Christmas, comrades."

Gunny passed the flask around a second time. They smoked their cigarettes. Then turned in for some sleep.

"Sarge, wake up."

He opened his eyes. "What is it?"

"We got visitors."

"How many?"

"Two…coming through the trees."

"Sentries?"

"I left Pace with the machine gun. Three more up on the hill."

"Alert the men to keep quiet. You there, snuff that candle."

"You, you, and you, come with me."

They stood inside the entrance and waited. Fifteen minutes passed. They heard talking.

Pasamenus whispered, "I think they're still looking for bodies and anybody still alive."

A head appeared through the cave entrance. He struck a match. Gunny knocked him cold with the butt of his Thompson. They dragged him inside.

"Tie this joker up and gag him."

A few minutes later another head came through the opening. Same procedure. Gunny crawled outside. He was back in ten minutes. "Coast is clear, prepare the men to move out."

"What about these prisoners, Sarge?"

"Got 'em tied good?"

"Yes, sir."

"Leave 'em. They'll work their way loose. We ain't murderers."

Ninety minutes later they were back where they had started the day before. The sun was just coming up, but there was still enough fog to conceal them a little while longer. The choppers were due any minute. Then they heard gunfire.

"Them bastards is loose, alertin' their buddies!" Then came the whomp-whomp-whomp of the helicopter blades. "Set up them M-60s on both sides of the road." One bird sat down, loaded, then lifted away. Another one sat down right behind him. "Demetri, you go with this bunch." His bird disappeared into the sunrise. Minutes later, three more Hueys settled down in single file along the roadbed. They loaded up and were away without incident.

Six Marines stood alone on the dirt road at the south end of the A Shau Valley as a vengeful mob of Vietcong guerrillas moved cautiously down Route 548. They were the survivors from the American bombing raid the day before. With them came a fresh platoon of North Vietnamese Army regulars who'd arrived that morning. The fog was burning away and the sun was shining through in patches. Images began taking shape up the misty roadway in the distance.

Seconds ticked by. "Steady, lads. He'll be along any minute now."

When the enemy soldiers got within 400 yards, Gunny had his riflemen lie down flat in the roadbed and release their safeties.

"Hold your fire. Don't look like they know we're still here."

"I could sure use one a Henry's prayers right about now."

"Damn right, hoss." Everybody was whispering.

"What if he can't find us?"

"Now there's an interesting thought."

"Steady, lads. He knows our location."

"What if he can't see us in the fog?"

"Back in The World, man, your old lady gets $10,000."

"Yeah, go buy herself a new Pontiac.

"Maybe get 'er one a them yard boys to trim 'er hedge."

"Mucho yard boys, three or four, maybe."

"You assholes."

Whomp-whomp-whomp!

"Let 'em have it!"

The M-60s opened up, sending twin streams of orange tracer fire streaking down the roadway. Four Marines with M-14s emptied their fifteen-round magazines. Screaming, yelling, return fire from a barrage of AK-47s.

"Load Up! Load Up!"

One Marine doubled over with a bullet in the stomach. Another Marine caught one in the leg. The machine gunners came running, cradling their weapons in their arms. Onboard, the door gunner let loose a hail of hot lead as they lifted away. The air around their craft filled with green tracer fire. Minutes later they were on their way to base, medical assistance, a hot shower, and roast turkey with cranberries and cornbread dressing.

Merry Christmas, Vietnam.

Chapter Twenty-Five

The Thing

The Elephant

"I want God to stop all that racket!"

Bubba was firing the M-60 machine gun in two- and three-second bursts, running the belts straight through, when Red tumbled into their sandbagged emplacement with four more boxes of ammunition. Red righted himself beside the assistant gunner to position his cargo, thinking oddly how the barrel was going to burn up, when a ricochet knocked the chin strap loose from his helmet. John was firing his M-14 in sweeping frontal bursts, emptying one magazine after another. All hell had broken loose. It was January 30, 1968. The North Vietnamese had attacked at 0300 hours.

"I want God to stop the fucking light show!"

Shrader was yelling at the top of his lungs as he slotted a fresh belt into the smoldering machine gun. It was his way of coping with the leaden fear that had them all by the balls. The VC and NVA were pouring out of the jungle in numbers far exceeding anything reported by Intelligence. Detonations rocked an eerie landscape. Rockets, Claymores, artillery…the flashes illuminated the grim faces of the men every few seconds.

"I want God to stop all that yelling and screaming!"

A dull crack by a 7.62 mm AK-47 round connecting with bone and tissue. The right side of Shrader's head became an ugly hole, splattering Bubba with warm blood and brains. John tossed his M-14 to Red, wrestled the twitching body to the rear of the parapet, then moved up to assist the machine gun. A near miss by an 82 mm Chinese mortar hurled a column of smoke and earth skyward, momentarily blocking out the moon. Over in the corner, a wounded Marine sat numbly thinking of all the things he had planned to do with his life but would never live to see. He died holding his intestines in his hands, his sightless eyes still staring at the hammering gun. None of them knew his name. A whispered prayer and Red scrambled over the sandbags, gone again for another load of ammunition.

A kill zone two hundred yards downhill had been cleared around the crown of Hill 509. Being the highest elevation in the area, it afforded the Marines uninhibited fields of fire by removing the trees and ground cover the enemy might employ for concealment. Dozens of Claymore antipersonnel mines had been set out around the camp in the outer edges of the barrier wire, which stretched back ten meters deep. Their fortified encampment covered the top of the ridge. Twenty meters back from the wire the company had positioned nine M-60 machine guns with interlocking fields of fire. A single battery of six 105 mm howitzers were positioned at the west end of the firebase. In addition, they had a .50 caliber machine gun mounted in the Observation Bunker built up ten feet above the compound floor. Command Center was underneath the Observation Bunker. The purpose of Firebase Hansel was mutual artillery support with Firebase Gretel, six and a half miles farther south and parallel to the Laotian border, and detection of enemy movement along the Ho Chi Minh Trail. Hansel and Gretel were under attack and fighting balls-out to stop the North Vietnamese from overwhelming their positions.

Red was dragging ass from humping it back and forth between his gun emplacement and the company's Ammunition Bunker. Now it was haul ass or die. God, for a drink of water, he thought. He was crouched behind a bulldozer to catch his breath, soaked with sweat down to his Marine Corps skivvies. "Lord, cut us a little slack down here, please."

The world had definitely lost its sense of humor as the Grim Reaper served up passports for Valhalla and Buddha's Promised Land. Scores of orange and green tracers streaked through the darkness, giving the illusion of jet-propelled fireflies zooming in all directions. Shells and grenades belched out colored lightning. Men fell and bled and died. The ground shook with one violent report after another. Flares popped, illuminating the escalating carnage. Each time Red ducked, his loose helmet bit into the bloody ridge of his nose.

"This one fo' yo' mama, suk-ah!"

Thoong!

Behind him an all-black crew were busily engaged manipulating an 81 mm mortar inside the safety of their sandbagged firing pit. Red watched with detached fascination as they went about their brutish trade with the practiced indifference of a minstrel show from hell. Shell fire silhouetted the faceless figures traversing the tube's elevation, left and right, backward and forward, rhythmically lobbing their high-explosive mortar shells high over his head so that they fell straight down, bursting red-orange in blossoms of ephemeral glory among the communist troops clawing their way up the hillside to get at the Marines on top. It was raining death in the razor wire. Something struck the hood of the dozer with a thump, bounced and landed at his feet. Red looked down to see a severed human hand.

"All kinda mangy shit comin' thru tha trees, man. Here one fo' you bad sister, sum-bitch. Right on! An' yo' nasty-ass cousins…an' Ho Chi Minh too!"

Thoong!

"Got tha fuckin' range, Jack! This one fo' yo' shit-ass Uncle Joe Stalin. Ha! Right on, muth-ah-fuck-ah!"

Thoong!

"I see ya! I see ya! Plenty to go round fo' all you crazy sum-bitches!"

Thoong!

"Hot off tha griddle, Jack!…Come on now…come on in an' get'cha one!"

Thoong!

Thoong!

A 130 sailed overhead, detonating 400 yards long and right, down at the base of the hill in the trees. Charlie had opened up with a 130 mm M-46 field gun somewhere back in the jungle. Another round came rattling in, landing 100 yards long and centered. They had the range. Then another high-explosive shell made its whistling debut, striking the top of the Ammo Bunker with a hollow BROOOM!

The mortar crew was raining 81s sixty yards front and center as dozens of VC and NVA troops sluiced through a breach they had blown in the wire.

On the east end of the compound, a twin-mount 20 mm motorized "duster" had taken a hit from a RPG-7 (rocket-propelled grenade) made in the USSR. All but one of the crew bailed out running. They carried the wounded man away with them. Hundreds of rounds stored onboard were caught in the fire and began exploding, showering the area with 20 mm projectiles. The calamitous din from hundreds of guns had become a monstrous fusillade.

Out of the smoke and purple gloom, a lone A-1H Skyraider glided in just above the treetops, his AIE switched on to image the body heat of the communist troops. Twin six-foot canisters of napalm tumbled from beneath his wings, striking the ground in no man's land with a jarring WHOOOSH as the jellied gasoline engulfed the running shadows. A dozen North Vietnamese Army regulars caught by the napalm became screaming fire beings from another galaxy. Their flaming bodies cast an eerie illumination as if in a satanic nightmare.

The south wall went nuts. "Crispy Critters! Crispy Critters!"

Communism versus Capitalism. Cain against Abel. Black Hats and White Hats. The East-West Titans were expending their sweet bird of youth in a dirty little brawl to establish who had the biggest set of balls in the equatorial jungles of the old French Colony. Up and down the South Vietnam countryside, the same twisted mano a mano masquerade was being played out beneath the power-lusting thumbs of Hanoi, Saigon, Peking, Moscow, and Washington. Politics. Ignorance. Greed. Power. Death.

It was the best of times and a real shit storm for others. Some of the best if you were smoking begonia weed and getting all the pussy you could handle back in "The World."

The pits if your were caught "In Country" in one of the Southern Provinces with your wang hanging out during the Tet Offensive. The old bureaucratic rim-job up the kazoo without benefit of K-Y Jelly.

President Johnson as Commander in Chief could best be described as a dud. His blind devotion to politics and cutting political deals kept him isolated from reality. He always believed Ho Chi Minh would make a deal someday. But Uncle Ho was a Vietnamese nationalist first, and a communist second. Ho wasn't interested in deals. Secretary of Defense McNamara was just as ignorant and stubborn as Johnson by refusing to loosen restraints on the ground war. Cambodia and Laos were placed off-limits, even though the Ho Chi Minh Trail ran the full length of both countries just inside their borders. North Vietnam was also off-limits, which made no sense militarily. General Westmoreland was an egocentric man in his own right, living in an elegant villa with executive furniture and a fancy Cadillac for a staff car. But he did have the military cognizance to ask permission from President Johnson to blockade the Ho Chi Minh Trail with three divisions, which might have ended the conflict. But LBJ and McNamara, fearful of world opinion and the possibility of China entering the war, refused to grant the general's request.

President Johnson did not want the American public to view him or his Democrats as weak on defense, yet he refused to unleash the American Armed Forces. And Secretary McNamara never got an actual grip on the military situation. So the war rolled on with no plans for winning, and no plans for bringing the troops home. The politicians in Washington had built themselves a tar baby.

Having never declared war, Johnson refused to extend military enlistments for a second term, thereby sending various units to Vietnam understrength because many of their best-trained soldiers were kept behind in the States. This misguided idea was to keep short-timers from going into combat and getting killed. To make matters worse, those who fought and became battle-tested veterans were shipped home after one tour of duty. Twelve months for the Army and thirteen months for the Marines—unless they volunteered to ship over for a second trip down memory lane with Charlie and the Pentagon.

The majority chose to go home because they saw what was happening. Hot pursuit of the enemy into Laos or Cambodia was not permitted, which was absurd, if not patently criminal. The best men were leaving every 12 to 13 months and being replaced by inexperienced soldiers, with no combat under their belts, and no training for jungle warfare.

Then there was that six-month limit on battalion and brigade command. The idea was to train more officers then rotate them out every six months, but in reality this hurt morale and cost the lives of a lot of good people. Meanwhile, the politics of South Vietnam was an ongoing soap opera of one failed coup after another.

The Pentagon was top-heavy with brass leftover from Korea and World War Two, which made for turf battles and countless petty mistakes. Serious mistakes too, such as building dozens of stationary forts in the South when the military should have been attacking points of origin in both North and South Vietnam, and across those neighboring borders into Laos and Cambodia. President Johnson believed in the Domino Theory, but he and McNamara never went for the knockout blow, only "communist containment" of the North, similar to Korea. The American Press began misreporting the war news in 1965, leaning more and more to their political Left, which never ended.

And Congress, as usual, was pulling in nineteen different directions all at the same inappropriate time.

"I'm outta here!" Red whooped, running straight across the compound...craters, shell casings, frightened men...flung himself flat to avoid a hail of tracers...ran, tripped and fell, got up and ran another 100 yards, then lunged through the open door of the Ammunition Bunker. And shelter from the guns. He knew without looking that the ammo handlers were dead. Shrapnel-gouged walls and that sickly sweet smell. Guts and blood. It always smelled that way. The 130 had blown off most of the roof, scrambling the two men inside like eggs with crimson yokes. It was a miracle the whole place hadn't blown sky-high. He grabbed up two boxes of ammo under one arm and a new gun barrel and a sack of grenades under the other, then ran like a scalded dog for the only safety he knew, cousin Bubba and his friend John.

The wreckage of the dead and wounded washed up everywhere, coming to rest piecemeal beneath the drifting magnesium flares. The Vietcong and NVA were piled up two and three deep all along the perimeter wire. American dead lay where they had fallen, the seriously wounded having walked or been carried to the First Aid Bunker. Those with lesser wounds remained at their positions, manning their weapons.

A Chinese 82 mm mortar scored a direct hit in the trench next to

John and Bubba. The four men over there were blown to hell and back. Nothing to send home but bones and body parts. Another round from the 130 gun came whistling in, blasting the Observation Bunker, killing a lieutenant and his sergeant. The .50 caliber machine gun tumbled to the ground, wrecked.

Bubba had shot away the heaped-up bodies blocking his field of fire, creating a bloody scene of gore resembling the lair of some terrible carnivorous creature. They came in waves from all directions, kill or be killed, giving it everything they had. Their last drop of loyalty and blood to overrun and kill the hated Americans.

Red landed in the bunker with the fierce cracking of bullets chasing his heels. The time was 0502 hours. The battle had been raging 122 minutes.

"Jesus! We thought you was a goner!"

"Don't say that! Anybody got some water?" He paused to catch his breath as a canteen was passed. "Best I can tell we're surrounded. They're all over the place." He paused again. "They blew the roof off supply. Third Platoon is catching it on the south side." Another pause. "They rolled a 105 over there, firing grapeshot point-blank."

John and Bubba looked at one another, then began assembling the new gun barrel. Red lay down on his back between the two dead Marines to regain his strength. A condemned soul peering up at a distant nebula, seeking deliverance from the Pit.

"How many clips you got?"

"Two. But the dead guy's got a sackful."

"Poor bastard. Grenades?"

"Seven frags...two Willie Peter...two Claymore."

"Gimme a Claymore. We got company next door."

"Cousin, I need a vacation!" Red handed the Claymore over to John.

John attached the wires then handed the device up to Bubba who poked it in the ground two feet out from their hole. John stuffed the attached detonator inside the magazine satchel to keep the contacts clean.

Artillery Platoon 177 had lost their number two gun to burned-out hydraulics. With 155 shots remaining, five men dead, and thirteen wounded, they were up against it. To conserve ammunition they were firing on a need-to basis. The 130 gun ten miles away continued to shell, but only intermittently. He, too, was running low on ammunition. The Skyraider expended the last of his 20 mm ammunition and flew away for base.

A battered enemy platoon had gained a precarious foothold on the east end of the compound. Close to seven hundred more were fighting savagely to join their brown-skinned brothers. The Tet Offensive was under way. A hundred towns and villages were under siege by 84,000 North Vietnamese Army regulars and Vietcong guerrillas. The American firebase at Khe Sanh was under attack by approximately 30,000 more.

A burst of machine gun fire sent John and Bubba sprawling down on top of Red.

"Commie rat bastards!" cursed Bubba.

"Get offa me and shoot that mother fucker." Red was being squashed.

"I'm telling ya, the dude shoots like a Marine."

"If you're havin' another identity crisis, get over here and let me have a crack at that sumbitch."

"Think you can nail his rice-happy ass, be my guest."

"Fuckin' A! Lemme in there!" John squirreled in behind the M-60 as Bubba slid around beside him to feed the ammunition belt. Red rolled over with his back against the wall to observe the proceedings. Bubba raised the flare gun and fired a round.

"He's down in a hole to the left of that big rock, about eight or ten feet."

"I kinda see where he is."

"Line up your sight about a cock hair above where you're gonna shoot."

"Two cock hairs. That's 700 yards."

"Yeah, I think maybe I was low."

The enemy gunner opened up again, sending a swarm of tracers and copper jackets crack-crack-cracking across the top of their sandbags. John spotted the muzzle flash.

"Son of a bitch!" exclaimed Red.

"Fuck him! Watch this!"

John adjusted the sights then squeezed the trigger and held it. Five seconds of 7.62 armor-piercing, copper-jacketed whup-ass hammered back at the enemy machine gun in Forth of July orange. Sparks and hot steel flew among the rocks on the hillside across from 509. There was no response. The North Vietnamese gunner had crossed the River Styx ass-end over chopsticks.

"Damn, son, you're a natural. Swing it around at them peckerheads over yonder in front of Fifth Platoon."

"Affirmative, dude."

John blazed away at the running shadows in the eastern sector with the remainder of his machine gun belt. A hornets nest returned fire. Bubba grabbed up the flare gun, firing an illumination round at the main concentration of muzzle flashes. White pop! Two figures sprang up, startled by the burning magnesium bouncing along the ground. Red shot them dead with John's rifle. Bubba let fly with an M-79 fragmentation grenade. It hit the ground short, skipped in the air and exploded, wounding two more VC.

Return fire became a storm. A fresh gunner on the hillside opened up with the Chinese machine gun of his dead comrade. Green meteors appeared to float across the valley, then shot around them violently. Gunfire was coming their way from three directions. Mushrooms of dirt and sand flew in the air all around Firebase Hansel.

Pasamenus ducked down low and took off running to scare up some seriously needed ammunition, leaving Marcus and a Marine buddy behind with their ARVN pal. Their ammo count was down to twenty-three magazines. No sooner had Pasamenus left than a wave of North Vietnamese flooded out of the trees at the bottom of the hill. The men up top opened fire. The ARVN trooper was using a new M-16 rifle.

Minutes later, the Marine on Johnson's right was struck in the center of the forehead, lifting off the roof of his skull. He took a step backward, reached a hand for Johnson, tried to tell him something and fell dead. Shaken by the grisly demise of his comrade, Marcus resumed firing.

The ARVN soldier, Bubby, was lobbing grenades as fast as he could pull the pins and throw them.

"Keep 'em comin', Captain. You're doin' swell. Throw us a long one."

Thirteen magazines remained. Then the Vietnamese boy caught one through the eye. Johnson held the young man in his arms while his lifeblood spilled out in the bottom of the trench. The boy didn't whimper or cry out, he just looked sadly into Johnson's face with his one brown eye until it glazed over and he was gone. Marcus repeated his boyhood prayer, taught him by his mother, as he positioned the limp body of his small friend against the right wall of their foxhole, beside the dead Marine.

> *"Now I lay me down to sleep,*
> *I pray the Lord my soul to keep.*
> *If I should die before I wake,*
> *I pray the Lord my soul to take."*

Vietcong were everywhere. Marcus fired at the running shadows with tears streaming down his cheeks. Bubby had been a happy, exuberant young man who wanted to move to America. Pasamenus and Johnson had planned to sponsor him. They called him Captain America, which thrilled the young Vietnamese and made him laugh.

He reloaded and fired another fifteen rounds. They fell in droves in front of his position. Others kept coming. Bullets were flying through the air, kicking up dirt all around Johnson's sandbagged foxhole. The last of his M-14 ammunition shot away, he picked up Bubby's M-16, fired three rounds, and the rifle jammed. Marcus flung it down the hillside, cursing the men who approved the new weapon, tossed his last grenade, then hunkered down for the blast.

When he looked out again, four of them were still coming. Wearing black short-sleeved shirts with black-and-white checkered neckerchiefs, brown pants, and rubber sandals. With fixed bayonets, they were crossing through a shattered place in the razor wire. He knew the enemy troops were out of ammunition because they didn't shoot him dead. Johnson stepped out of his hole and stood his ground, waiting for them, a dead man's machete in his hands. They had killed Kevin and Bubby. All the men around him in four foxholes were dead. Dead Marines and ARVN bodies littered the east end of the compound. Thirty-two enemy soldiers lay at his feet and down the hillside. Marcus had reached that stage in combat where he was operating on pure adrenaline. Mentally, he had made his peace with God and was prepared to shake hands with Jesus Christ, Saint Peter, whoever was manning the Pearly Gates. Better him, he thought, than Pasamenus. He would kill these sons-a-bitches or go down fighting like a man. A proud Southern black man.

Running along the south wall, Gunny Abernathy was a welcome sight, carrying a load of bandoliers around his neck, a satchel of grenades in his left hand, and a tommy gun in his right. He knelt down on one knee, tossing a bandolier and a grenade to a trooper waving to him from a foxhole. Two more Marines stood up yelling in the hole next door. Two more bandoliers were shucked off his neck. Gunny hurried on. He was delivering his hardware to a machine gun bunker when a bullet knocked him off his feet. Two men rushed out and dragged him inside.

The first Vietcong approached in the classic bayonet stance. The wiry man lunged. Johnson slapped the rifle aside, bringing the machete down hard, severing the man's arm above the elbow. He struck him again in the neck, and the man went down gurgling blood. A second VC rushed Marcus. Johnson ducked, slicing the man across the face and down his belly. The enemy soldier dropped his weapon, stumbling into Johnson's foxhole, clutching his guts in his hands.

Finally, his luck ran out. The third VC nailed him, pinning him against one of the poles supporting the corrugated metal roof over the foxhole. The bayonet went through his left side, deep into the cypress wood. Johnson swung the machete down viciously, burying it in the top of the man's skull, but he was stuck fast with the rifle protruding out front of him like some terrible phallus. And the last Vietcong was approaching with blood in his eyes.

A potato masher grenade landed at Red's feet. "Sweet Jesus!" He grabbed it up and flung it away as hard as he could throw it. Then a pineapple grenade bounced in.

"Gangway!" John grabbed up that one with both hands, hurling it down the hillside.

So much ordinance was flying through the air a man could hold up a Lucky Strike for a light.

Over in Command Bunker, the first lieutenant was conferring with Captain Abraham. A decision was reached. "BROKEN ARROW." The radio message went out. Firebase Hansel was in jeopardy of being overrun. Every available aircraft in their vicinity would begin stacking up at thousand foot intervals, awaiting instructions on where to deliver their ordinance. Four aircraft nearby began radioing Captain Abraham of their estimated times of arrival. The Skyraider was back, so that made a total of five. Every available airplane and attack helicopter in South Vietnam was in the air or being serviced and armed due to the massive attacks taking place up and down the countryside.

Johnson could not pull the bayonet free, so he bent the rifle sideways until the blade snapped in two. Excruciating Pain! He fell to the deck with the enemy soldier not ten feet away. Marcus struggled to get back up but fell over a dead man underneath his feet. He rolled then, expecting the blow. Shots rang out. One! Two! Three! The enemy soldier toppled over on top of Johnson with a surprised look on her face…it was a young woman with close-cropped black hair, wearing a little blue-and-red flag pinned to her left breast pocket. Pasamenus was by his side, tending to his damaged comrade.

"I'm sorry, Marcus. It took forever to find what we needed. They're dead aren't they? I'm sorry it took so long. Can you walk?"

"How many times you saved my black ass? Two? Three? I ain't sure no more. One thing I am sure about. I'm glad you weren't here, Eshkhan. You might be over there with Bubby and them dead fellows. God rest their souls. Let's get the hell outta here."

Red peeked out for a quick look. Moans from a wounded man to his left were heartwrenching. "Cover me, guys. I'm goin' out."

He flopped over the sandbags and crawled to the pit where the sound was coming from. Before he could utter a word, a VC sprang out of the hole, slashing his arm with a dagger. Red blew him away with three shots from his .45, then crawled back to his foxhole.

"Gunny warned us about that. That sucker got me good!"

John wrapped the wound with his T-shirt, then bound it tight with Claymore wire.

Pasamenus and Johnson came tumbling in, followed closely by PFC

Gonzales. Then Gunny landed in the pit on top of the dead Shrader. Driggins dropped in. Living quarters were going for a premium that holiday season. The compound was a quarter mile long and 400 feet across in the middle, with foxholes every 60 to 75 feet dug in around the periphery. Some with fortified log emplacements, others had corrugated metal roofs. All five Marines had just scrambled through two hundred yards of flying steel from the eastern perimeter, which was collapsing under the onslaught. Two more stragglers crawled in. Then another orphan appeared with a bloody shoulder wound.

Gunny was more the concerned father now than top sergeant. "We're calling down an air strike, so stick close and follow me to the 105s. Keep low. I don't want none a you gettin' hurt. Hug the deck. Somebody gets hit, drag his ass. I'll keep my eyes open for Mister Charles. No need for alarm. We're doin' fine. Check your weapons, lads. Make sure you got full clips. Smith, you bring the machine gun."

He held out his hand to them. It was covered with blood. Without saying a word each man clasped Gunny's hand, then they set out on their perilous journey across the open battle terrain to the presumed safety of the howitzer pits. The wounded man had lost so much blood he finally passed out. Johnson and Pasamenus pulled him along between them. Johnson was leaking blood himself, but Pasamanus had patched him up around his middle with a Red Cross bandage and a roll of Duct Tape. By the time they were halfway to the gun pits they were done in, so Red and Henry spelled them. Gunny was out front with his Thompson submachine gun, with Bubba bringing up the rear with the M-60 gun and the ammo belt draped around his neck to keep it out of the dirt.

A Chinese 82 mm mortar landed behind them with a muffled BANG in the loose dirt of the pit they had just abandoned. Then the 130 mm came spiraling in, detonating in the eastern sector where the communist troops were gaining their foothold. Automatic weapons fire cut through the compound, peppering Command and the First

Aid Bunker, ricocheting off the bulldozer, and clanging against the blast shields on the howitzers.

The carnage of war lay scattered everywhere. Shell casings, arms, weapons, legs, bandages, mangled bodies, wooden crates, rolls of toilet paper, cartridge casings, the company flag blown off the Observation Bunker, and burning fuel drums meant for the helicopters.

Continuous rifle and machine gun fire, mixed with the blasts of the cannons and exploding mortar rounds, made it impossible to hear out in the open. Men were struck by shells and blown apart like melons. Claymores and rocket-propelled grenades exploded up and down the line, blasting hot metal into yielding flesh. The wounded on both sides lay in crimson pools of suffering and dying. The sun was coming up. The fog was lifting. It was going to be a beautiful morning.

Gunny spun sideways, crashed to the deck, then hobbled back on his feet with a bullet in the hip. One of the newcomers caught a 7.62 through his side. His friend grabbed his cartridge belt, hauling him upright to keep him moving forward. A spent round hit Bubba in the forehead…down he went. John and Pasamenus pulled him back up. John took the M-60 machine gun, firing continuous bursts at the muzzle flashes at far end of the compound. Finally, they were inside the sandbagged security of the 105 guns. There they found sixty-plus men hunkered down in the howitzer pits. Nearby foxholes were just as crowded. Everywhere, the ground was caked red with blood.

Minutes ticked by before the last stragglers finished coming in. Then Gunny made the call to Command Bunker. He talked while a Marine medic applied a bandage to his bare butt.

"That's it, captain. I checked ever' foxhole out there."

A Phantom jet nosed over from two miles up, making his bomb run on the black- and brown-clad figures he could see at the east end of the firebase. At 2,000 feet, he released two 750-pound fragmentation bombs, then banked hard right amid streams of tracer fire streaking up to greet him. Two terrific detonations, followed by columns of black smoke. Next came two Skyraiders flying abreast. They roared in over the compound at two hundred feet, releasing four canisters of napalm which struck the east end, flashing down into the trees. Men came running out of the woods on fire. They ran until they collapsed and burned and died. A Cobra gunship flew down the south side of the compound, methodically firing his 2.75-inch rockets into the tree line. A second Cobra flew along the north side, performing the same lethal operation.

Each Cobra was equipped with twin rocket pods carrying a total of thirty-nine rockets, plus a single 7.62 mm electronically fired minigun. For the next twenty minutes, each aircraft took turns strafing various stretches of ground around the camp. The miniguns made nails-on-the-blackboard screeching sounds when firing. Then they were gone.

The A-1Hs were the last to leave, having expended the last of their missiles and 20 mm ammunition into the trees. An eerie silence fell across Firebase Hansel. No sounds, except the popping and cracking of the burning fuel drums and the moans of the wounded.

Gunny ordered his men to fill their canteens from the water buffalo, and to take care of the wounded as best they could. He assigned Second Platoon the task of distributing the remaining ammunition from the Ammo Bunker. Third Platoon assembled the dead from the general area in a long, bloody row. Body parts they stacked like cordwood.

The rest went to work squaring away their dugouts and firing pits, tossing out anything that might get in the way or hinder their ability to fight. Then Gunny told everyone to break out their C-rations and grab some rest. He knew from past experience more was yet to come. Then he set about the task of checking the gun emplacements and their crews, encouraging those young men he found with long faces. Gunny was shot in two places, but looking after his Marines took first priority.

First Squad lay huddled among the minstrel gang in the 81 mm mortar pit. Soon they were sawing logs. John dreamed about Samantha and buying a new home. Bubba dreamed of raising a son with his beautiful Suzie. Command Bunker in front of the sandbagged howitzer crews was still operational, but the First Aid Bunker in the center of the compound had been blown to pieces by a direct hit from the M-46 field gun. Everyone over there was in God's hands.

Signs of a renewed attack began with the shrill sounds of whistles in the forest. A bugle tooted from the top of Hill 507, a neighboring elevation 158 feet lower than Hill 509. The time was 1330 hours. Enemy mortar rounds began making their wearisome appearance again. A couple of enemy machine guns opened up, and twenty-five to thirty AK-47s began chattering away, but it wasn't nearly with the ferocity of the night attack some ten and a half hours before. Captain Abraham radioed the airmen who were rearmed and regrouped, following their second strike that morning at Firebase Gretel. Firebase Hansel was about to receive a squadron of five Skyraiders who were on their way, and a single chopper loaded with munitions and medical supplies.

The 105s fired shots of white phosphorus, indicating where some of the Chinese mortars were buried in the hillside so the flyboys could synchronize their bomb runs.

The first A-1H came down at 45 degrees, releasing his payload at 500 feet then pulling away, skimming the tops of the jungle. Napalm hit the trees, splashing down in a boiling circle of yellow flames, followed by secondary detonations. A second A-1H bore down in the same manner, releasing his payload. Again, secondary explosions. They were toasting something of value. One black-clad VC ran out of the tree line covered with flaming napalm. Then a third fighter bomber delivered his canisters of jellied gasoline.

As the last two aircraft flew across the compound at two hundred feet, Hill 507 erupted with everything but the kitchen sink. A trap had been sprung. The North Vietnamese had a .57 mm antiaircraft weapon firing straight into the Americans from the top of the ridge.

Muzzle flashes appeared up and down the hillside. Tracer fire filled the air around the two aircraft. The outboard plane exploded in midair, cartwheeling end over end down the hillside in a billowing fireball. The second pilot managed to release his bomb load, but was trailing white smoke badly so he headed for the barn. Men watched in horror as his plane belched flame once, rose up in a stall, then nosed over in a slow roll, crashing down into the jungle. A mighty cheer went up from Hill 507.

"Turn them guns around, boys." Gunny was on the radio with Captain Abraham. "AA battery on top of 507. Request air strike, captain."

Abraham acknowledged but the flyboys were already forming up for their attack. They blasted the length of the ridge, knocking out the .57 gun, but a heavy concentration of enemy forces still remained on the hillside. And Firebase Hansel had already sustained 50% of her company of 247 men either killed or wounded.

The Huey helicopter, carrying the much-needed ammunition and medical supplies, began his landing approach from the south side of 509, while the A-1s were plastering 507 on the north side, when its tail rotor was shot off causing it to spin down into no man's land at the bottom of the hill. The pilot and crew never made it to safety. They were cut down only yards from their aircraft. And there was no way the Marines could reach the site before nightfall, perhaps not even then. They could see their supplies, but they might as well have been in Saigon or on the moon.

For the following thirty minutes the three aircraft expended their missiles and 20 mm cannon shells into the face of 507, while the Marines fired the last of their 81 mm mortar rounds at targets that were plainly visible. Now only six shells apiece remained for the five 105 mm howitzers. Enemy rifle and machine gun fire continued unabated. Bubba had a belt and a half left for his machine gun. Three other machine gunners had seven belts between them. Red and Henry and the majority of those still in the fight were down to five or six magazines apiece. "SITUATION IN DOUBT" went out. Toots and whistles in the trees indicated another attack was forming up.

Marines are warriors like every soldier in every corner of the world, even before Samson declared war on the Philistines. Some are better than others. Roman Legions were excellent soldiers. So were the Greeks, the Huns, and the ancient Arabs. But Marines have an esprit de corps ingrained in their ranks which bonds them together spiritually. They will lay down their lives for a comrade. This is not to suggest that the Army and Navy or the Air Force don't have their share of brave gladiators. Marines are just different. Semper Fidelis (Always Faithful) is more than a mere statement by Marines. It is the very core and essence of being a Marine. For God and country means just that. They are the alpha and omega for defending Lady Liberty and Uncle Sam.

Pasamenus gazed out across the ragged circle of men, some wounded, others dying, with a great sense of sadness and fierce loyalty. None of them had broken. They had fought heroically to a man. They had fought and died like Marines. That was something, considering they were outnumbered three or four to one. Still, he wished he might have seen his mother and father one last time. They were so proud of him when he enlisted in the Corps. Now it seemed such a miserable waste. Intelligence had bungled the job. The generals were equally guilty. The war was being manipulated and lost by lawyers and politicians sitting around in air-conditioned offices and boardrooms back in Washington. He was going to die with Marcus, Gunny, and all his friends. That made him angry as hell. This was stupid beyond words. He felt a terrible sadness for his parents. Sorrow, too, for the others' parents.

The morphine helped a lot. Johnson was thinking about Alabama and the night he scored the winning touchdown for his high school team, which sent them on to the state finals. They got their tails kicked, but it was a memorable experience. And mama. She would mourn her only child, whom she had taken to church almost every Sunday those eighteen years they lived together. Tears rolled down his cheeks as he remembered his sweet mama. He wished he could do something to save Pasamenus, John, Bubba, Red and all the others. That seemed like a dream now. They were about to die in a stinking jungle, fighting a bunch of assholes whose names he couldn't even pronounce.

Gunny had lost too much blood to remain standing, so he took a position propped up against the sandbags with the howitzer crews. His calming voice kept the men occupied with their assigned duties. The lieutenants were all dead. A number of the wounded could no longer hold a weapon. Gunny cradled the .45 caliber Thompson in his lap. He knew they were up the proverbial creek, but he was not afraid to meet God. He smiled to himself, knowing how sad, and happy too, Sun Li would be with his insurance money. He would check out for that big veteran's plantation in the sky knowing he had made a difference by training young Marines how to fight and survive in battle.

Captain Abraham came running across the open space from Command, where the radios were housed, to consult with Sergeant Abernathy. "Pat! Hang on, old fellow. Puff is twelve minutes ETA."

Out east a silver speck gleamed, caught by the glare of the afternoon sun. Something dreadful was approaching from the coast in the direction of the surrounded Marines, not unlike the apparition John had seen in his nightmare so very long ago. Slowly it grew. Then came the drone of the engines. Finally, they could see it, the sinister blue hulk of an AC-130 gunship looming larger and larger by the minute. They stared, mesmerized, as the pilot banked his plane up 30 degrees on her side. Straight in she came, at 6,000 feet over the top of Firebase Hansel. A shaft of light appeared from the ship down into the jungle, accompanied by the thundering howl of explosions. Hill 507 began disintegrating under the electronic scream of two 20 mm Vulcan Gatling cannons, one 40 mm Bofors cannon, and one 105 mm auto-loading howitzer. Trees, rocks, guns, people, were blown to bits as the precision-driven beast maneuvered her terrible weapons across the enemy positions.

"Oh, my God! Look at that! Look at that!" Red was jumping up and down.

Captain Abraham helped Gunny to his feet so he could see. The men were standing and cheering. The United States Air Force was decimating the North Vietnamese forces surrounding Firebase Hansel.

A 15-year-old farm boy, forced into service by the Vietcong, felt the ground tremble and shake, and the horrible screams of the dying behind him. An earthquake was rumbling his way at 120 miles an hour. Instinctively, he wedged himself into a hog burrow underneath a moringa tree. Earth and chunks of wood and leaves showered down, burying the boy as a wave of exploding munitions and flying shrapnel swept the forest floor above him. Digging his way back out, he found devastation. Shattered trees, branches, and broken bodies lay everywhere. Men had been blown into the trees and hung there, suspended like Tet decorations for the new year, blood dripping down on the aftermath of the AC-130 gunship. The ground was cast about as if plowed by oxen driven mad by the Americans.

It was both beautiful and terrifying to watch. The jungle seemed to explode in wide swaths as the four-engine, prop-driven gunship made pass after pass around the firebase. High above, two F-104s flew cover in case any MiGs tried messing with their blue fat lady. The east end of the firebase lay pulverized. The face of Hill 507 was soon shot to hell. Part of the valley on the opposite side of Hansel looked as though a tornado had plowed through it. One final sweep, pounding the top of Hill 507, and "The Thing" waggled her wings a fond farewell. The fat lady had just sung her grand finale.

Chapter Twenty-Six

The Garden of Eden

Gunny was on the mend, so he wrangled a two-day pass for himself and First Squad. It had been seven weeks since the battle at Firebase Hansel. The division was reinforced and back up to strength, rested and refitted. It was time for a little diversion before they went back in the field with a newly arrived herd of green jarheads. Gunny was intent on getting his boys laid.

Dwayne Henry had received the bronze star and his corporal stripes for wasting a sapper squad of bad guys, then carrying a wounded corpsman from one end of the compound to the other, which saved both their lives. He was shot in the legs while doing so and lost a couple of toes in the process.

Top wanted him in his menagerie, telling the religious corporal, "The Lord won't mind a little pussy for one of His heroes."

Corporal Henry thought about that one for a spell. One of his buddies was dead, three others were there in the hospital with him and

Gunny. One of the new boys lost both his legs. They were out in the courtyard catching the rays. Red and John were out there with them, Pasamenus and Driggins. Marcus Johnson was recovering nicely. Bubba still had a scarlet knot on his forehead were the bullet had fractured his skull. Gunny had his right arm in a sling. Dwayne Henry cogitated over where life had taken him, away from his unhappy existence in New York City to this distant place of healing in a war-torn part of the world filled with peasants and people trying to kill him.

These young men. These Marines. They were his family now. His real family, a true brotherhood of men. Comrades of war. Tested in blood and sweat and valor and tears. They would never fail him nor betray him in any way, and he knew that. He looked up at Gunny with his close-cropped red hair and crooked grin, Pasamenus with his friendly but inquisitive eyes, John and Bubba and Red, the Tennessee Hillbillies. Men he called brothers. Driggins and Johnson, two more he would trust with his life. Had trusted at death's door. God had placed him there for a reason. He didn't know why or much care anymore. He might even die there, but he knew he would follow these men into hell if they asked him to go with them.

"Yes. I may not partake of the ladies, but I'll go with you. I'm one of you now."

Gunny looked down at Corporal Henry sitting in his wheelchair in the sunshine. Then he said something that caught them off guard. "Yes, you are, corporal. You boys are the sons I never had. I am proud to have known and served with each one of you. I hope all of you make it back home safe and sound. America is going to need young men like you once this stinking war is over."

Then he told his Marines about their two-day liberty pass.

Red could barely contain himself. "Hallelujah, brothers! We're goin' to the candy factory for loose wimmin! Big Red is a buckin' an a snortin' just thinkin' 'bout them baby dolls. I can barely keep the varmit in my britches. Say, Gunny, sir, how much is this gonna cost us?"

"It's on me, Red. My New Year's gift to you jokers for a job well-done."

"Far out! We look like a herd a Christmas presents all wrapped up an ready for delivery." Red was proud of their smart appearances.

Bubba and John chuckled at Red's gleeful enthusiasm.

"Will there be big-breasted hooter ladies?"

"Pasamenus, you're gonna think you're at the Moulin Rouge in Paris."

The hospital at Da Nang was twenty minutes drive from The Garden of Eden. They arrived by taxi, armed to the teeth, with new boots and freshly starched uniforms. None of them, besides Gunny, had ever been to a cathouse before. Corporal Henry was the only virgin in the group, followed closely by Pasamenus who'd experienced one brief roll in the hay with the eldest daughter of an olive farmer in Italy.

Outside, the place looked like a dump. Inside, it was elegant. Candelabras with mirrors and heavy tapestries, paintings of the kings and queens of France and England. Portraits of Charles de Gaulle and Winston Churchill hung above a magnificent mahogany bar arrangement. Franklin Delano Roosevelt was up there alongside Ike Eisenhower, Bernard Montgomery, and Erwin Rommel, the Desert Fox. The lights were low, the carpeting plush, and the furniture imported from India. It was a regal setting fit for boardroom executives. A meeting place for gentlemen. Madame Mimi appeared in the arched doorway to the dining room.

"Lucian! You old devil dog!"

"Mimi! You Parisian heartbreaker! I've missed you!"

"Give me a hug, darling. I, too, have missed you." They embraced. She kissed him then hugged him again. She felt the bandages. "Are you hurt? Are you injured?"

"A few scratches here and there. I want you to meet my boys. Some of the finest fighting men I ever soldiered with."

"They look so big and strong. But so young, Lucian, must they be so young?"

"I was young once. Remember?"

"You were handsome too, and always trying to get in my panties."

"You seduced me, you wench. They may look young but they saved my patoot."

"You sweet man. Come sit. Drink with me. What may I do to make them happy?"

"Jackson and Smith there are married. Faithful married. Have your attendant serve them. Henry here would like a glass of champagne. Pasamenus is the brains of the outfit. A smart one for him. Red over there, and Johnson, the big one, played football. They're good Southern boys. Driggins is from the East coast. Something sweet and salty for that one, my dear."

Gunny handed Mimi an envelope. She rose, placed the envelope behind the bar, then tugged a decorative cord hanging beside the wall. An attendant appeared, dressed as a French maid, to take their orders. Another tug and the door at the top of the stairs opened. Down came a bevy of females. Ten very sexy females.

Henry dropped his rifle.

"At ease, corporal. They ain't gonna bite ya."

Madame Mimi laughed. Everyone laughed. The ice was broken.

The girls mixed and mingled while the boys enjoyed their drinks. Mimi spoke to her ladies in French, explaining to them what Gunny had just told her about his men. A busty black-haired beauty touched Pasamenus's shoulder, speaking to him in Tai and broken English. He listened intently, then surprised everyone by speaking to the Tai lady in French.

"Mon Dieu, he is the Brain!" Madame Mimi rattled off a long litany of French, answered by the Armenian in like fashion, causing her to cry out. "Ooh la la! His mama and poppa, they are the patriots too!" She leapt to her feet and hugged Pasamenus.

Then she rattled off another broadside about her father fighting with the French underground against the Nazis. Pasamenus told her of his poppa's similar exploits. They laughed merrily and hugged again. Gunny and his boys, Mimi and her girls, everyone was delighted with their playful antics. A party ensued. Thoughts of the war and dying and being so far from home soon evaporated from the room.

Corporal Henry was in awe of the women, all of them pretty. The Tai girl talking with Pasamenus was gorgeous. A small, attractive blonde sitting beside Driggins was holding his rapt attention discussing Oriental koi. Red had disappeared upstairs with not one, but two hay-market queens, another redhead like himself, and a shapely brunette. The rest were gathered around John and Bubba at the dining room table, with Gunny and Madame Mimi holding court. Corporal Henry was resting on an ornate sofa in front of a marble fireplace, enjoying the fire and listening to a German girl relate her tale of how she came to be there.

Her husband had been French. A captain with General de Castries at Dien Bien Phu. He had survived the battle, but died along the 300-mile march to the prison camps. Half the French prisoners perished during those three months they spent in captivity. They were all used up from the terrible ordeal of fifty-five days of relentless fighting. At the very end they had no food, no medical supplies, no ammunition, and no hope. It broke her heart. Madame Mimi found her drunk in a bar in Quang Tri and took her in. She was never asked to work as a prostitute. Then one day she did, hoping it might help her to forget, and to repay Madame for her kindness. After that she never looked back. Corporal Henry put his arm around Sophie, holding her close as one might comfort a long-lost sweetheart.

The Tai girl had three years of college at Bangkok University. International Diplomacy, she laughed. Her fiancé had been killed at the battle of La Drang, fighting for the communists. It seemed everyone in the room had lost friends or loved ones in one kind of war or another.

She told Pasamenus about the history of Vietnam, how it had become the graveyard of invading armies for the past 2,000 years, even before the time of Christ. She loved his mind and told him so. Soon, she was leading the Brain up the coveted stairs to a rendezvous he would never forget.

Johnson had discovered a Vietnamese firecracker. She was spirited and gay, reminding him of a majorette he knew in high school. Su Su spoke good English. Then she would lapse into Vietnamese, and Marcus would roll his eyes. She felt his musclar arms, giggling, praising his manliness and his ability to sire many sons. Su Su genuinely liked Johnson.

She asked him about the race relations between blacks and whites in the United States. Marcus explained how things gradually had been changing since President Eisenhower was elected in 1953. He told her about the racial beatings, lynchings, murders, separate restrooms and drinking fountains, and Irene Morgan and Rosa Parks. And the strides made by President Kennedy and Martin Luther King Jr.

Su Su wanted to know if Gone With the Wind was really about the Old South. Marcus told Su Su about his great-grandfather, Solomon, who had been a slave on a cotton plantation in Georgia. When General Grant marched on Atlanta, Solomon Johnson fought on the side of the Confederates. Johnson was the name he took from the plantation owner. His mother came originally from a small village on the coast of Cameroon. Solomon was nearly killed by a Yankee miniball, but a Union physician dug it out and saved his life.

They were seated at the mahogany bar, serving themselves, both a little giddy from a bottle of schnapps. Johnson gazed into her black eyes, beautiful black eyes. A circuit blew out inside his head, dredging up dark memories.

…He was running down a red football field…the players chasing him were the ghosts of dead men…they were running in blood. He flung the football away…it burst in blue stars, then his gaze soared up into the clouds over the battleground. He was at the Mickey Mouse Club at the Strand Theatre. John and Bubba were on screen firing a machine gun. Explosions…blue stars…Goofy was chasing Pluto… Sergeant Kohn was there showing them how to parry a bayonet thrust. A man lunged…he had black eyes…then the dual-mount 20 mm exploded. Another man rushed in…that man had black eyes. His mother was crying because she couldn't afford a Christmas tree. The blade went through just above the kidney…IT HURT!…Mickey Mouse was over and it was getting dark and he was scared…he slumped to the ground…Gunny was screaming at him to get up…the Vietcong raised the bayonet. Mama arrived…little Marcus ran and hugged his mama…

"Honee? Where you are? You go away and leave Su Su. I miss you where you gone. You come back now? Maybe I say something make you feel bad? I sorry. You okey-dokey now, OK?"

"I'm cool…I'm…I'm A. J. Square Away." He paused. "I was thinking…about…it's gone now." Marcus was experiencing post-traumatic stress. "We're here, baby girl. Here in this boo koo fine place. I'm happy as a ole piggy in a mudhole. You're Number One. My Number One girl."

"I like you, Meester Johnson. You nice man. Number One for me too."

A couple of schnapps later, Su Su led Johnson up the stairs to her room where she undressed and bathed him in the tradition of her people. They made love. Then they talked about the war until they felt the urge again. Finally, they fell asleep in one another's arms, sleeping the night away like two contented children.

Madame Mimi invited her bouncer to join the gathering around the dining room table. Gunny liked him immediately. The feeling was mutual. The man was tall, lean, well-muscled, with dark skin, and wearing a black leather eye patch over his left eye. Madame introduced him by an odd name, Gargoyle. A former sergeant with the French Foreign Legion.

"Do you mind being called that?" asked John.

"Because of my face? No. The scars, I have them all over. Compliments of our friends from the North. They caught me and two others trying to sneak through to the guns in the hills overlooking the valley. We were going to knock them out with thermite grenades. Luck was not with us that day. They killed my friends. They left me for dead."

"That musta been something."

"Oui. I remember the screaming. Then I realized it was me. Later on, an old villager found me. He saved me. I send him money when I can. Sometimes Madame gives me extra to send. It helps his village. They are very poor but a wonderful, proud people. When the war is over, I may go there and live. But I will remain here as long as Madame needs me. I am too ugly to go home." He chuckled, taking another sip of his cognac.

Madame Mimi touched his arm, telling him tenderly that he was a beautiful man inside. The Legionnaire adored Madame Mimi, ever since she bailed him out of trouble following a barroom brawl where a man was killed.

Gunny leaned forward, elbows on the table, looking intently into the mutilated face. "You can always come with us. Legionnaires are welcome. We could use a man who speaks languages. The Corps makes a fine home for old salts like us."

"You are most kind, mon ami. We may talk again of this matter when the war she is finished. But tonight, we drink. To Absent Brothers."

"To Absent Brothers!" They raised their glasses in salute. Madame Mimi rose. They all stood, with glasses held high to the dead.

The Gargoyle felt a camaraderie he had not experienced since his glory days with the Legion. That night he acquired a new blood brother and a new family of warriors, Gunny Sergeant Abernathy and his young leathernecks.

The party continued on with the merrymakers drinking and laughing. It was indeed a grand and magical evening for these noble crusaders, destiny's heroines and heroes. Servants for God and country. At 3 a.m. the party broke up and they retired to their quarters.

A bomb blast rocked the neighborhood an hour later. Everyone rushed out into the hallway, half-dressed, then flocked downstairs and out onto the sidewalk to see what was happening. A police station two blocks away had been blown up and was burning, black smoke and orange sparks billowing up in a fog-shrouded night sky. Ambulances and fire engines came screaming around corners. A truckload of South Vietnamese soldiers passed by. Gunny told everyone to get back inside lest they get murdered by the same bunch of assassins.

That scare settled Corporal Henry's dilemma. He followed Sophie back upstairs and settled himself in bed with her. Next morning, no one spoke of the event. They knew what had taken place between Sophie and the corporal was something special.

Day two of their liberty pass was delightful. Madame Mimi spoiled everyone, her girls included, with special treats, caviar and champagne, even fried chicken with mashed potatoes and gravy, which she had coaxed Private Johnson into telling her was his favorite meal. Gunny was puffing on a Havana cigar when Madame came into the parlor.

"Lucian, would you step outside and help me a moment?"

Her surprise was a Christmas tree, a fluffy little three-needle pine. Gunny assured Mimi it was perfect for the occasion. They set about decorating the young pine tree, with John and Bubba helping before the others came down from upstairs. Once the lights were plugged in, it was indeed perfect. It reminded the Americans of home and happier times around other Christmas trees, while outside, a few kilometers away, rode the Four Horsemen delivering holiday packages no one wished to receive.

The Americans controlled the cities by day. They also controlled the skies over Vietnam. But Charlie ruled the countryside by night. Eighty-five percent of the population resided in the rural areas, so not much was being accomplished in the way of influencing the minds and winning the hearts of the people. Whenever the Americans showed up, the VC would simply vanish. Then, when the Americans left, the Vietcong would come back out again. More than one-third of the villagers had been uprooted in a forced relocation program by 1968, including those left homeless by the fighting. The people resented it.

Gunny knew what was next on his agenda, but he had mixed feelings about telling his men.

Chapter Twenty-Seven

Madame's Courtyard

"I had that dream again."

"What dream?"

"Dipano driving the car."

"I wish you'd stop dreamin' that ape-shit. We got troubles enough without you blowin' a head gasket."

"Sergeant Kohn and Sergeant Bear were in the backseat. They come and got me off the playground, just like before."

"Maybe you ought to see the Brain and ask him. Or go over to Section Eight and have your crazy ass checked in for a lobotomy."

"I'm serious…an' you're fuckin' with me."

"All right, but them crazy dreams you're havin' don't make no sense a-tall. Tet was a mother-fucker, man. We're lucky to still be alive."

"Don't I know it. I can still see those jokers comin' up the hill."

"I can't believe we killed all those Vietcong."

"Red done good, didn't he?"

"Damn straight. An' Johnson, an' Henry. We all done good, bro."

"Robert, if I say something weird, you ain't gonna think I'm queer or nothin'?"

"No, but I know what you mean. Gunny said something about it at the hospital. He said combat brings men together closer than wives and family. He said it will last the rest of our lives."

"I guess he knows, all right. I never felt like nothin' special before."

"We'll make it back OK, long as we stick with Gunny and the others. You miss Sam?"

"I miss that girl every day of the week."

"I been dreamin' about Miss Suzie."

"We're lucky, man, even if we get blown away over here. We're lucky because we got each other, Red an' Gunny, an' First Squad, and we got our ladies. That's more than most people have in a lifetime"

"It ain't like the old days, that's for sure. I didn't have a brain back then. All we ever did was get drunk and chase women. Things sure have changed. We belong with these Marines, man."

"Can you believe we're in this place, not jumpin' their bones?"

"Sure can, dude. We got two of the finest women on the planet waitin' for us back in K-Town. I wouldn't trade that for a thousand uh these mama-sans."

"Right on, Bubba. I got no interest in none a this. All I care about is Samantha."

"When I get home, I'm gonna drive Suzie around that bedroom like a danged wheelbarrow!"

"Both us, man. I love Sammy so much, sometimes I just sit back and thank God."

Chapter Twenty-Eight

The Mission

The afternoon sun finally broke through the clouds, falling across the parlor room floor in long rectangular patches through the leaded-glass windowpanes. The golden sunbeams upon the teakwood floor reminded Gunny of a time more than twenty years ago when he was a young Marine onboard a troopship in the Philippine Sea. The sun was shining down through the clouds that day too when a torpedo tore out the bottom of a troop transport a mile up the column. She turned turtle and went down in minutes. He remembered all the men in the water when they cruised by them not more than fifty yards away. He and the others wanted to stop, but the captains of the invasion fleet were under strict orders not to stop for survivors because of Japanese submarines. Two Australian destroyers returned the next morning, only to be sunk by a Japanese wolf pack.

Gunny's .45 caliber Thompson sat propped against the wall beside his easy chair. Madame's cook had just served green tea. Finally, Gunny spoke.

"Listen up, men. I met with Major Abraham before we left. He asked me to pick a few good men for a special assignment. It's dangerous, so this is strictly volunteer stuff. There's a commie sumbitch near a place called Base Area 611 at the north end of the A Shau Valley. It's rough terrain up there, and the place is lousy with gooks.

"Intelligence been tryin' to locate this asshole for months, but no dice. He's a cagey one. He's also a fucking sadist. His men will capture one of our people then he goes to work on them. They specialize in officers. A man can only stand so much, then he spills his guts. That's why their ambushes have gotten better lately. He squeezes it out of some poor bastard, then they know our plans. But it doesn't stop there. He does sadistic things to the men they capture. Our CIA boys been findin' some pretty gruesome stuff lately.

"Intelligence doesn't know his name or what he looks like, but they have a description from a CIA operative who spotted him from half a mile away. Our guy was up to his ass in VC at the time, so he never got off a shot. But he told Intelligence the man is six feet tall, big for a Vietnamese, about 175 pounds. And he was wearing a white scarf around his neck. Word from some of the villagers confirms that white scarf.

"Some of you men went through sniper training at Parris Island. Whoever volunteers, if any of you choose to do so, I'll be leading this parade. It won't be easy, so no hard feelings if none a ya go. There is a perceived weakness in this Base Area 611. There's a four hundred foot cliff in there full of caves. Lots of ground cover. Intelligence thinks that's his base of operations.

"The plan is to create a diversion a few clicks north from where a helicopter will put down the sniper team. Bombers will be blasting Area 611 while our gunships are laying down fire all over the place. One quick chopper landing should do the trick. If the shit hits the fan, the Mayday call is "Philadelphia." A dozen choppers will be on standby in case my team gets in trouble.

"I don't blame none a ya if you don't go. It's a tough assignment. Do I have any volunteers?"

Johnson spoke before the others could respond. "Just one thing, Gunny. If we make it back with our nuts still attached, will you bring us back here again?"

"That's affirmative, Marine!"

They stood, to a man, each in turn clasping Gunny's hand. Nothing more was said. Marcus Johnson had said it for them. There was a mission to perform against a sadistic murderer. But, first, there was good food to be enjoyed, more vintage wine and excellent spirits. And the charms of some of the finest hot patooties in Viet-by-god-nam!

That night, Madame Mimi invited Gunny into her bed, sensing he was troubled about something. His relationship with Sun Li, their ongoing union of convenience, was placed on hold for the evening. She gave the master sergeant her love, hoping he would survive. Hoping she would see him again. Hoping in her heart of hearts she would see them all again.

Chapter Twenty-Nine

The White Scarf

B-26s and Cobra gunships were pounding the crap out of the mountains up ahead when they touched down seven clicks south of the cliff. Five seconds on the ground and the chopper pilot was up and away. Before them lay a green maze of double and triple canopy, bamboo, green undergrowth, and fog so thick they couldn't see fifty feet in any direction.

Mosquitoes swarmed up to greet them. The bug juice helped, but not enough. Flies too, big green ones grown fat from feeding on the carcasses of dead men. Henry was the first to notice the leeches. John watched in disgust as the long, sinister-looking creatures rose up several inches, weaving about, testing the air, sensing their presence, then down they went, crawling toward the men. It was 0700 hours and already the heat and humidity indicated a hot day ahead.

"What a comedown this is from where we was two days ago."

"Yeah. How can a place look so nice and be such a pain in my ass?"

"Pipe down. We could step on one a them bastards in this soup."

They followed the top of a ridge that led them in the direction of the cliff. Each man would disappear into the fronds, followed by the next man. The fronds clutched at them, embracing them with multiple leaves and branches, slapping them in the face when they moved forward too quickly, followed by the wait-a-minute vines that tangled in their weapons and packs. They proceeded through a green maze of shadow and suspense. Insects were everywhere, accompanied by the real possibility of getting killed around the next tree. Half an hour later they took a break to get their bearings and swallow some water.

The fog had lifted somewhat, so it was becoming easier to see. Gunny studied the map then handed it to Pasamenus. The men gathered around to determine their location. That was a trick Gunny had learned on Guadalcanal. If he was killed, they could find their way back on their own. It had saved his life once before.

Pasamenus spoke while Gunny listened. "Looks like about four miles, sir. I suggest we follow our ridge to this dogleg a mile and a half or so, then take the high ground on the right, then down this ravine beside the creek, then up the other side until we come abreast of the cliff."

"That's good, Pasamenus. That's real good. Henry, you take point. Keep them eyeballs clickin'. We're ass-deep in Charlie country. All right now, move out."

They continued on to the dogleg, then switched off right until they came to the ravine when Henry held up his hand. Something was bugging him. Gunny moved forward to reconnoiter.

"Right there, Sarge. See it?"

"Good job, son. Somebody don't want us crossing their creek."

Two separate tripwires shown black laden with moisture from the morning fog. Henry stepped on a leech and squashed it.

Gunny studied the map, locating another ravine farther ahead. Then he handed it to the others to study. With Gunny on point, they arrived at the second gully twenty-five minutes later. The ravine was grown over with bushes and vines. He crawled down partway before he was satisfied.

"Looks like two hundred yards to the bottom. Then it levels out on both sides of the creek. Not much vegetation on either side, flash floods probably. Don't make no noise. Not any! If this place was mine, I'd have lookouts posted."

At the bottom, sure enough, they spotted a sentry. The man was asleep. Gunny crept out into the water until he was chest deep, approaching the sleeping Vietcong on the far bank. Just as he had trained them, half his men were watching upstream, the other half watching downstream. Gunny was on top of the VC just as the man heard the dripping water, hand clamped over his mouth, a trench knife rammed into his heart. The North Vietnamese kicked a few times in his death throes then slumped back, dead.

They hid the body in the undergrowth then advanced up a steep slope until they reached a well-traveled path on top. The undergrowth there had been cut back, making it easy to walk. A double canopy of trees overhead made it impossible to be seen from the air. A few yards further on they spotted another sentry. Gunny motioned for Driggins. The range was 100, maybe 120 feet.

"Can you do it from here?" Gunny whispered.

"I think so. I'll steady on that limb over there."

Driggins rested the barrel of the Smith & Wesson .38 revolver on a mossy branch, cocked the hammer, sighted carefully at the man's head, then slowly squeezed the trigger. The silencer went "pomp!" The man toppled over dead with a bullet in his brain. They stashed the body in the bushes and moved on.

They had covered another 300 yards when Pasamenus noticed something strange about the foliage on their immediate left. He held his hand in the air and they stopped, motionless, in their tracks. The Armenian crept forward, feeling his way along the vines and leaves…

and chicken wire! Then he saw it, an opening. A narrow doorway. Just inside sat a third sentry, seated on a wooden crate reading a magazine, an AK-47 across his lap. Pasamenus and Gunny whispered back and forth, then Pasamenus reached through the opening, yanking the man off his crate and pulling him outside. Two trench knives delivered him to Buddha Land before he could sound the alarm. Pasamenus crept inside. Minutes later he was back.

"You will not believe this place. We found it!"

Inside, they discovered tents, a wooden table, chairs, a cooking grill, great mounds of boxes covered with blue plastic, and flowers. Beautiful jungle orchids hung all around the interior. The proprietor loved orchids. The compound was 150 feet long and 100 feet across, with camouflage netting doubled and tripled overhead and around the sides. No way could it be spotted from the air.

And right in the middle, suspended between two trees, hung the burned corpse of an American. He was naked except for his boots. They had built a fire under him. His GI boots were burned black, as were his legs and charred private parts.

"Don't touch anything!" Gunny was furious. They were all bent out of shape. "We'll wait for that white-scarf cock-sucker! Get on both sides uh that hole. Use your knives! Driggins, use that revolver if they show up in a herd. The rest a you, no shooting unless you absolutely have to."

Gunny went to search the tents and see what was under the plastic.

"Hear that? Somebody's coming!"

Two sentries strolled in and were immediately pounced on and dispatched. Ten minutes later another one walked in, only to have his throat slit by Bubba while John and Driggins held him down on the deck. Blood splattered their fatigues, giving them the appearance of butchers in a jungle slaughterhouse.

Sarge returned with a handful of GI dog tags and an NVA codebook. Then they heard whistling. Someone was approaching the doorway with not a care in the world. They spread out and waited. It was him! The man they had come to kill, white scarf and all. When he saw them, he panicked, screaming and fighting desperately to flee and escape, but it was too late for happy rice-pudding endings. He screamed and fought them every foot of the way as they dragged him inside, pounding and kicking the man senseless. There they bound and gagged the sadist.

They tied him against one of the trees supporting his flambéed American entertainment, next to the ashes of the fire White Scarf had personally built and supervised. The Vietcong had driven bailing hooks from cargo ships through the American's wrists, then strung him up with wires attached to the handles. The sadist had wrapped the man's torso with razor wire beneath the arms, which dug into his ribs every time he kicked and screamed with the flames searing his legs and but-tocks. Cries were heard that night far down the valley while the sadist chuckled to himself, whistling his little tune, sipping his rice wine, and tending a slow fire underneath his struggling victim.

"Men, I don't go in for this kind of thing, but this dirtbag needs to pay some dues before we part company. Any suggestions?"

They went through a gamut of ideas until Red mentioned the leeches. John and Bubba nodded to Gunny, Gunny nodded back, John and Bubba hurried outside. Minutes later they were back with two helmets full.

"Strip him, underwear, shoes…make sure he ain't gettin' loose." Johnson found gloves and a pair of wire cutters on the table. Cutting a piece from a coil, he wrapped a strand of razor wire around their terrified guest until he resembled a piece of his own diabolical artwork. Blood ran down his chest and onto his naked belly. The leeches sensed the blood and began crawling from the spot where John and Bubba had dumped them out on the ground. The man's eyes rolled insanely as they approached his exposed thighs and penis. Each time he squirmed, more blood dribbled down. Corporal Henry said a prayer before the suspended American, then walked away and sat down at the table. Then he threw up.

"Get back and watch that hole. Pasamenus, you come with me."

The men stood guard beside the entrance while Gunny pulled the plastic off the boxes. Rifles, grenades, ammunition, mines, tons of the stuff. Explosives for making booby traps. There was enough ordnance to supply a regiment for a month. And boxes and boxes of rice.

Patrick carefully inserted four detonator caps in four separate bricks of C-4 while Pasamenus threaded twenty feet of fuse together, which would give them twenty minutes to hightail it before the whole thing blew.

Finally, they stood before their dinner guest one last time.

"You're a good-for-nothing commie son of a bitch. Now you're gonna die like one, pissin' an kickin' in your own filth. But first we're gonna kill a few more minutes while your little friends there finish their supper. How's it feel to be on the receiving end, asshole?"

Gunny kicked him in the mouth, twice, smashing the man's lower jaw. Blood poured down. Pasamenus nodded his head in approval. They smoked their cigarettes while the leeches sucked and filled their bellies. The sadist tried to scream for help, for mercy, gagging on his own blood, his eyes rolling in his head like a be-crazed animal. But the dead American's sock taped inside his broken mouth made that an unrequited chore. The Marine Corps scales of justice had weighed the man, judged him guilty, then sentenced him to the Pit.

"Time to go!"

Pasamenus coiled the long fuse among the boxes, covering them with the blue plastic to hide the smoke in case somebody walked in before the C-4 detonated. Then he lit the combined fuses and out the door they went.

They made the creek and were scrambling up the narrow ravine when the mountain behind them lit up in a boiling fireball resembling an atomic bomb. The ground convulsed violently as bits and pieces of earth and broken timber showered down around them.

"This ain't no time for snoop and poop. Dump your gear, run like mother-fuckers."

They kept their weapons and ammunition, shedding their packs and helmets, then they ran. Two wearisome miles through the trees, sudden gunfire silenced the noisy palaver of the birds and monkeys. Henry fell to the ground, clutching his chest. The Marines opened fire…one dead sniper. Henry was hit in the lungs. Leaves and twigs began flying around them from gunfire coming across the narrow valley.

"Johnson, make that call!"

"Philadelphia! Repeat. Philadelphia!"

"We receive you loud and clear, Red Dog. What is your position?"

"One mile north of rendezvous. Repeat. One mile north of rendezvous. Dust Off! Di Di Mau! Dust Off!"

Johnson adjusted the radio on Pasamenus's back, then picked up Henry in a fireman's carry. John and Bubba emptied their weapons across the valley at the muzzle flashes on the hillside. Then they lit out for the rendezvous point.

"Shit's getting deep, Sarge. We ain't gonna make it with Henry."

"I know that. Keep them eyeballs clickin' for a chopper place to sit down."

The vines and fronds made it hard for Johnson carrying the corporal. His face and hands were scratched and bleeding. They were all beginning to drag ass from humping it through the thick foliage and high humidity. Finally, Gunny was on his last legs. For the first time in his career, he wondered if maybe he was getting too old for cutting the mustard with young men half his age.

"Gimme a minute…get my breath. One of you, scout ahead. Jackson you go."

John took off to recon the forward area. Private Johnson laid Corporal Henry down on the jungle floor to tend his wounds. Marcus was bleeding in a dozen places and flat-out exhausted. Pasamenus stuffed his sweaty T-shirt inside Henry's fatigue jacket to help stem the bleeding. Henry was unconscious.

John reappeared from the greenery, dripping with sweat and out of breath. "There's a clearing. It's big enough. They'll have to come down through the trees...100 yards...it'll work."

Behind them they heard dogs for the first time. Pasamenus radioed that they would make purple smoke. Estimated time of arrival was twenty minutes. The dogs were getting louder. Bubba scooped up Corporal Henry, then made tracks. Gunny took out a tobacco tin from his fatigue pocket, sprinkling a substance all around the ground where they had rested, then followed his men into the dense undergrowth.

The attack aircraft arrived first. Driggins popped a smoke grenade so the choppers could see them. Cobra gunships began firing into the jungle. It was reassuring, but they were a long ways yet from a cold Pabst Blue Ribbon. The tracking dogs let go with howls of pain. Red pepper had found the mark. More gunfire. Rounds began snapping twigs and leaves above their heads. Gunny radioed the pilots to hit the trees behind them.

The gunships took turns blasting the jungle with rockets, firing more than 450 missiles in the time it took for the rescue helicopter to arrive, land, and pick up the men.

Red pepper had saved the day, saved their by-god asses. A few minutes later they were flying over the south end of the A Shau Valley. A commie rat bastard had been sent upstairs to Comrade Lenin's hacienda in the clouds. Several commie rat bastards had made the trip. Corporal Henry was on his way to a hospital in Da Nang with a million-dollar wound, which was his ticket back to The World.

Not bad for a day's work. Not too shabby at all.

Chapter Thirty

Sophie

As promised, Gunny treated them to another night of slap-and-tickle at The Garden of Eden. Madame Mimi cancelled a prior engagement after Patrick called, asking if he could bring over his six Marines for the night.

"But what of the other boy?" she asked.

He explained what had happened in the boondocks, telling her Corporal Henry was in the hospital, badly wounded. Madame wrote down the name and address. Later that night, she informed Sophie. Next morning, the German girl hailed a taxi to go see her corporal. When Gunny and the boys arrived at the Garden, Mimi explained what she had done. Three more taxis were summoned. Everyone loaded up and rode off to the Dust Off Inn.

When they arrived in front of Corporal Henry's door, Madame and Gunny peeked in through the oval glass. There in a hospital chair beside his bed, holding Henry's hand, sat Miss Sophie. Henry had a breathing tube up his nose and the usual bells and whistles stuck in one arm, but he was out of the woods after his doctors had removed two bullets from his chest.

Corporal Henry was delighted to see them. Still doped up a little, he beamed when he saw Private Johnson. The last thing he remembered before passing out was bouncing through the trees on Johnson's shoulders.

"Thank you for saving me," he whispered.

"You'd do the same thing for me. On second thought, I'm too damn big."

The room heehawed.

The girls crowded around, giving the corporal kisses. Madame placed a box of chocolates on his nightstand, then his comrades gathered around the bed wishing him a fast recovery and joshing him about being a goldbrick and chowing down on pogey bait.

Henry beckoned for Johnson's hand. "Thanks for carrying me."

"I ain't the only one, bro. You wore me slap-out, so Bubba took over. Man, you weigh a ton!"

"Thank you, Robert. Thank you all for my life. A man couldn't ask for better friends than you guys. You too, Gunny. Thank you for getting us out of that awful place alive."

"Just doin' my duty, corporal. But it was a little tight, wasn't it?"

The head nurse came in, informing them that the girl could stay but the rest of them were too much excitement for her new boyfriend. They said their good-byes and left.

Regretful and afraid, the blonde German girl sat holding the American boy's hand when tears began streaming down her cheeks. She wished with all her heart, all her feminine soul, that she was good enough for this fine Christian man. But she knew she wasn't. If only she had been stronger when her husband died. Now it was too late for her. She knew she could love Corporal Henry. Sophie wanted so very badly to love him, but he could never love her. She wondered miserably if her life was ruined forever. She was used merchandise. A lowly prostitute. If only she had been stronger, she thought. If only she had remained a lady.

"Why, God? I'm so ashamed. Please forgive me…God, please." She began to cry brokenly.

Corporal Henry stirred from his morphine-induced slumber, gazing into her pretty blue eyes and running mascara. "What a lovely mess you are," he whispered. "Would you like to have children, Sophie?"

Sophie lay down her head on the side of the bed and kissed his hand. "Yes, my love. You dear, wonderful man."

For the second time in two weeks, Mimi invited Patrick into her bed. She was experiencing emotions long dormant since their love affair fourteen years ago. He had been on the staff with a Marine Corps general in that bygone era, visiting Vietnam to determine the damage done against NATO and the United States by the French tragedy at Dien Bien Phu. Her feelings disturbed her, more so than she wished to acknowledge. Yet she found herself longing to see him again.

That night, when the others were in bed asleep, she clung to the master sergeant . "Lucian, I worry about the boys. I worry about you too."

"We did a good thing out there, a noble thing. We killed a degenerate bastard."

"I heard them talking downstairs. You were lucky in your escape, were you not?"

"I'd do it again if they asked me."

"What if you become the one killed? I would become the woman most sad."

Lucian turned to the French beauty lying beside him. She smiled back at him, but not as she had the week before. Something about her had changed. She looked radiant lying there in the moonlight. A feminine goddess. She reached over, touching his face. Lucian kissed her brow, her lips, her breasts. He wanted her so badly it consumed him. They joined, Mimi holding him tightly in her arms, whispering sincere affections in her language of love. The sergeant rode her savagely to those distant heights where only ecstasy dwells.

"Oh, Lucian. My darling Lucian."

The following afternoon, the boys said their good-byes. Everyone had enjoyed a marvelous time. A special bond had been struck with these Marines. The ladies liked them best out of all their customers. And so it came to pass for Madame. No longer was she a woman for hire. She just ran the place. But her affections for Patrick Lucian Abernathy had spilled over again. The girls could tell something was different, but they didn't know what. Madame had changed. The master sergeant appeared the same. Yet he, too, was quieter, not his usual jovial self.

As the taxi pulled away, Mimi Le Beau stood on the sidewalk, waving good-bye with her little silk handkerchief, smiling sadly with tears in her eyes. "Adieu, mes cheries. Que Dieu vous garde."

Chapter Thirty-One

Quang Tri

May 1968: They were conducting a search and destroy operation along the Ben Hai River thirty miles west of the South China Sea. Just north lay the Demilitarized Zone. Behind them were Laos and the Ho Chi Minh Trail. South was Quang Tri City. Fourth Platoon had been in the boonies twelve days, working their way east. The men were tired and dirty, and held a mangy resemblance to the creeping crud.

A large enemy force had been reported west of the Hien Luong Bridge, so they were up there snooping around for the Air Force. Two minor firefights had occurred over a ten-mile search area, with one man killed and eleven wounded. Those individuals were dusted out and taken back to Da Nang. They had four confirmed NVA kills in regulation army uniforms. No VC had been sighted following Tet. Still, they had not yet located the main enemy force.

A tropical storm blew in from the ocean, and that's when things got amusing. Gunny set up a defense perimeter, then took off his fatigues in the middle of the circle and began washing himself and his clothing in the rain.

"All right, you bilge rats. Get them duds off and start scrubbin'. We're Marines, not a herd uh stripe-ass baboons. Wash them feet good. Put fresh socks on if ya got 'em."

It was funny as hell seeing all those guys with lily-white bodies scrubbing away with sun-browned necks and hands. They resembled white monkeys without any fur, just brown necks and faces. Of course, Johnson wasn't white, but he added to the comedy by being black all over which made the rest of them look anemic.

Red threw his soap and hit Bubba on the back of the head. A wrestling match ensued, whereby half the platoon ended up covered with mud, while Gunny sat naked on the sidelines, laughing his ass off. It was good to be alive after all they'd been through those six fun-filled months since they landed at Da Nang. Brave men they had known and shared good times with and fought beside were dead. Others had been shipped home with crippling injuries. Corporal Henry had elected to rejoin Fourth Platoon after he and Sophie tied the knot at the hospital. Gunny gave her away. Madame Mimi filled the hospital room with flowers and an assortment of gifts. Sophie cried and cried but she was the happiest girl alive.

Scrubbed and still wet, they bivouacked back in the trees for the night. Red pulled out his little transistor radio which picked up Saigon really well. Sarge let him play the thing so long as he kept it down low so Charlie couldn't hear. Procol Harum came on with "A Whiter Shade of Pale."

> "We skipped the light fandango
> turned cartwheels 'cross the floor
> I was feeling kinda seasick
> but the crowd called out for more
> The room was humming harder

as the ceiling flew away
When we called out for another drink
the waiter brought a tray..."

John interrupted. "I like that song. There's something about it that's awfully sad. Those guys sound like they're singing about this place."

"Perhaps they are, John. Perhaps they are singing about Vietnam."

"It sure is melancholy, ain't it?"

"Yeah, it's pretty cool."

"Pipe down guys, I wanna hear this."

"...And so it was that later
as the miller told his tale
that her face, at first just ghostly,
turned a whiter shade of pale..."

Red interrupted his own reverie. "This is killer, man. Makes me wish I's back home with one a them 38-D Hose Queens."

"...If music be the food of love
then laughter is its queen
and likewise if behind is in front
then dirt in truth is clean..."

"Brain, what's it mean 'if behind is in front'?"

"I read an article last year in Esquire about "The Peter Principal." I believe they're singing about our cultural disintegration which, too, embodies the principle of employees being promoted to their level of incompetence. A man can be good at one job, but when he's promoted to the next level he's in over his head. Government is the only enterprise in the world that expands in size while its failures increase."

"Say that in English, hoss." Red was an apt pupil.

"Well, some members of Congress are incompetent at their jobs. Quite a few, actually. They get elected, same as being promoted, because they look good or say the right things, what people want to hear. Then they're in over their heads. The same is true for any profession. The best physicians are good because of intelligence. The worst members of any trade usually embrace the bottom rungs of the social ladder. Regarding society, the Left Wing is attacking the old schools of thought. And, as you already know, the Pentagon has its fair share of incompetent generals."

"That Left Wing stuff. You mean them war protesters?"

"Yes, but some good may come from that, which remains to be seen."

"I never heard it put that way before. But is society disintegratin', really?"

"Some, yes. The New York Times printed the story "God Is Dead." Certain people promoted it for all the wrong reasons. They proposed that man created God in man's image, not that God created man in His. The founding fathers were mostly Judeo-Christians. This addresses the issue that part of our society is drifting away from our roots."

"I ain't driftin' no place. I'm with Henry on this one. If I die out here, I'm goin' to Heaven. I believe that."

"So do I, Red. I believe we'll all be in Heaven someday."

"I'm glad you believe it, Brain. The men look up to you 'cause you're smart. Believing in God is important to them. It is to me too."

"I'm flattered you feel that way, Red. I do my best to be a good Marine."

"I know, hoss. I knew it back at Parris Island."

Johnson and the others sat listening to Red and Pasamenus talk about God and "The Peter Principle" for another half hour, then turned in for the night. Red put away his radio, and they lay there awhile staring up through the open spaces in the trees. The sky was deep purple with a million stars shining down from above. And for once, the mosquitoes weren't so bad. Before falling asleep, Red wondered about God and why so much misery existed in that part of the world.

Dawn came with Gunny going from man to man, waking them and signaling for quiet. Something was going on beyond the trees. The men crept forward through the ferns and bushes, then switched off their safeties. Right there, about seventy-five yards away, were 25 to 30 sitting ducks preparing breakfast in an open field. They had no clue that Yama, the lord of death, was watching them from the trees. Whatever they were cooking sure smelled good.

It took Bubba less than a minute to get his M-60 machine gun belted and set up on its bipod underneath a tangle of vines, while the others got down in comfortable firing positions with their M-14 rifles. Driggins and another Marine were using M-79 grenade launchers. Then all eyes turned to Gunny and Lieutenant Butler.

Lieutenant Butler was a good man. He'd been in Hue during Tet. Gunny liked him, so that was good enough for the platoon. Lieutenant Butler nodded…Gunny raised both arms in the air…then dropped them. They opened fire.

It was over in a minute. Twenty-six guns blazing away at enemy troops at point-blank range was as easy as shooting targets at Parris Island. They lay in bloody piles all around their cooking fire. The official count was twenty-seven NVA killed. Luckily, the cooking pot was still standing upright. While Gunny and the lieutenant searched through the pockets of the dead Vietnamese, John and Bubba took the rice stew back into the trees, picked out the dirt kicked up by the firefight, and everybody ate breakfast.

Once Lieutenant Butler and Gunny had finished and rejoined the platoon, the men learned the NVA troops were all teenagers, with the exception of their older commissar. Little wonder they had been so careless. Hanoi was scraping the bottom of the barrel following the Tet Offensive. Gunny walked over and dropped something in Bubba's hand. It was a ruby ring he had taken off the dead commissar. Suzie was going to get the gem Bubba had promised her. They finished the rice stew, then the platoon saddled up and headed east. Corporal Henry said a prayer as they walked past the dead youngsters.

The majority of that day was spent making their way through the jungle. Hot and humid, snakes and lizards. It was easier going near the riverbank with the mangrove trees and crocodiles, but Gunny and the lieutenant kept them in the boonies most of the time to avoid being ambushed. They didn't know what was out there, so they stuck with their Jungle Jim routine. The men couldn't see ten yards in some of that stuff, but they were safer in there.

Midafternoon, they emerged from the jungle at the base of yet another hill where only grass and bushes grew. Lieutenant Butler took off up top to see where they were. Partway up, he disappeared in a tall grove of trees. Then he was back, motioning for the men to join him.

From the crest of the hill they could see for miles down a long, wide valley that ran parallel with the river toward the sea. It was a beautiful green valley with double and triple canopy on both sides and grassland out in the middle. They had emerged from the jungle on the side of a high ridge, sloping down 1,500 feet to more jungle at the bottom. There was a dirt trail out there with a creek beside it. On the far side and back a ways was a great burned area where a B-52 bomber had fallen from the sky. Patches of green were growing here and there among the wreckage.

"I know where we are, sergeant. That bomber is seventeen kilometers from the coast. They went down last November. It's marked here on the map. We're less than five kilometers from the river. What do you think about this spot as observation for a day or two?"

"Good thinking, lieutenant. Good visuals. Easy to defend. We see them assholes we can sic the flyboys on 'em."

Chapter Thirty-Two

Red Dog Down

The Cat

At 1700 hours they were busy digging out their C rations when a cat wandered out of the boonies and sat down between Gunny and the lieutenant. The men didn't know if they would kill the critter and cook it, or what? The lieutenant picked up his trench knife and reached inside his pack. That's when Corporal Henry rose to his feet, on the verge of presenting the Pussy Defense.

Then Butler sliced the top off a tin of sausages and gave one to the cat. Then he gave one to Gunny. Then another sausage to the cat. The lieutenant ate just three sausages, with Gunny and the cat chowing down on the rest. From then on Lieutenant Butler was aces in everybody's book.

The cat was black all over with two yellow hind feet, so Henry named her Boots. Boots took over the camp, with everyone giving her bits of food from their rations or the extras they carried in their packs. It was like old home week with a kitty cat wandering around camp and no one shooting at them. That night, on the hilltop, was the first time in thirteen days they felt halfway civilized. It was peaceful up there. They even had a breeze. And Red had his radio.

Pasamenus was the equivalent of a walking encyclopedia. He informed the circle of men that most modern-day cats were descendents of ancient Egypt.

None of them had ever met anyone like the Armenian before. He certainly was a lethal character, full of contradictions, but one of the nicest men around. In some ways he was like Henry, religious and all. Other times he reminded them of Sarge, a leader of men but ruthless when situations arose. The platoon always felt better when those two were around.

The elevation took them up above the mosquitoes for a spell. Each time out, those pests appeared in squadrons. If it hadn't been for the bug juice, they'd have carried them off in the trees for supper. The humidity sucked, big time. Each man had lost between five and ten pounds, and their feet were usually wet from walking through the jungle. Some of the Marines had trench foot. When they changed their socks patches of skin peeled right off. Still, they were managing pretty well, and the flyboys were on standby in case they got their asses in a sling.

Boots was still with them the next morning. She looked pregnant from all the goodies she'd eaten. Everyone liked the little cat, but Lieutenant Butler had taken a real shine to her. So had Sergeant Abernathy. The men watched with growing admiration as the two professional Marines displayed playful affection for a tiny creature which, often as not, landed on the menu in Indochina. Watching their leaders play with the cat reminded them they were still human and not the brutal, dope-smoking killers they were portrayed to be by a biased and uncaring media.

Sarge and the lieutenant decided they could do more good where they were for a few more days, so they ordered foxholes dug in case Charlie came a-courtin'. It took the men until midday because of all the roots. Cutting through a tree root with an entrenching tool and a machete was a pain in the ass, but they had one double-bladed axe, so the men took turns chopping. Driggins's hole, with Gonzales, was three feet deep. With ponchos spread across the top, they would be warm at night.

Driggins came from a small town called Yaupon Beach, North Carolina. He told Carlos Gonzales about the sea turtles. His father was a Marine biologist, and his mother helped pop with his research. Fred worked summers at the resorts, and also helped his father with his work. There's a place near Yaupon Beach called Bald Head Island. There's an old lighthouse there. That's where the loggerheads came each summer to lay their eggs. Fred and his mother always tried to save as many baby turtles as they could when the babies made their run for the ocean. They used firecrackers to chase away the birds. But there were too many birds, which kept eating the hatchlings, no matter what they did. So one morning Driggins and his mother smuggled a 20 gauge shotgun out on the island. Bye-bye birds. They buried a couple of dozen in the sand dunes so they wouldn't get in trouble. The rest of that summer the birds flew away whenever they showed up on the beach.

His dad had been wounded at the battle of Saipan. Pop told Fred about the Japs taunting them at night. "Hey, Marine, you mama dirty whore! You die tonight, Marine!" He said they were good soldiers but often used poor military tactics. Banzai charges just got them killed. Said their navy was better than ours in the early months of the war, but after the Battle of Midway our guys got the upper hand. Driggins was going back to Wake Forest when he shipped out of the service.

That night there was a full moon but no stars, due to a haze overhead, but they could still see well enough up and down the valley. Somebody was down there, but they couldn't tell who it was. Two campfires appeared in the darkness. One, way the hell east, and another one straight across from them. It was spooky with the fog rising off the creek and those fires glittering down below. Were they friendly tribesmen? Or the Vietcong? John sighted his starlight scope on the campfire across the valley but all he saw were five silhouettes. The platoon remained quiet that night and ate their C rations cold.

Next morning they were gone. Lieutenant Butler searched the valley floor for an hour with his binoculars but didn't see anything. Gunny suggested sending out a patrol and the lieutenant agreed. They picked Carlos and Fred and John and Bubba to go down and check it out. They left their gear behind except for their rifles and ammunition, and the platoon's twenty-four empty canteens, which they carried with them in two field packs.

Bubba led the way, backtracking through the jungle, then working his way west a quarter of a mile before they started down the mountain. Down on the valley floor they didn't see anything at first except the usual trees and elephant grass. But once they got to the creek bank and filled their canteens, they found boot prints and impressions left by rubber sandals. Not good. Charlie had been there, NVA and VC.

On the far side of the trail John discovered an empty rice tin left beside the ashes of last night's cooking fire. Definitely not good. Those bastards were using the valley. The four young Marines hightailed it back to camp and gave their report. Gunny and the lieutenant agreed. There was enemy movement in the valley. They doubled the sentries and waited.

That night more campfires appeared. This time there were eight fires back west of them a little over a mile. The skies had cleared and they could see by the light of the moon. John put his starlight scope on the scene and, sure enough, there must have been a hundred and fifty or two hundred down there. That was way too many for local tribesmen, and no friendlies were in the immediate vicinity except Fourth Platoon.

Lieutenant Butler radioed the enemy position to the Air Force who were on standby awaiting his transmission. Forty-five minutes later, the valley floor lit up like a Christmas tree. Napalm, white phosphorus, high explosives…the whole thing lasted fifteen minutes. They could feel the air concussions and the ground quaking from the bomb blasts. Then they flew away leaving behind them a scene from Dante's Inferno. The sentries watched the fires and the smoke rising until dawn. Lots of popping and cracking as the ammunition burned. All those screams they heard that night gave rise to a serious case of limp dick. Getting shot or blown away was one thing, but being burned to death was something else. Eternity hung in the air that fateful night and that awful wail of souls freighting starward.

Sunup, they could see clearly dozens of bomb craters and the blackened fingers of earth where the jellied gasoline had splashed and ignited among the enemy troops. A hundred or more lay dead, mutilated and burned. More were injured. It was a sad situation for the enemy soldiers because they were such a long way from any medical help. Then they heard the gunfire. They were shooting the critically injured. It was the humane thing to do. They would have died along the trail, anyway.

Lieutenant Butler addressed his men after chow, although several of them had lost their appetites. "What you people saw last night was butt-ugly. War is a revolving shit storm. A Class-A bitch. In all wars, the side that kicks the most ass wins. Today we are the victors. Those poor bastards down in the valley are yesterday's news. Butch up, Marines. Those fuckers would kill you in a heartbeat!"

Lieutenant Butler understood how they felt about the napalm. Maybe he felt that way himself, but his little pep talk did the trick. It was far better to be on top of the mountain than a cooked goose down in the valley.

"Reckon them's the ones we come out here huntin'?"

"Could be. They sure was a lot of 'em."

"Makes ya glad we own the air, don't it?"

"Fuckin' A! Gettin' wasted with napalm is the rag, man."

"Wonder how many got killed?"

"Seventy-five, a hundred maybe. Charlie knows we're here, though."

"You reckon?"

"The sky falls on your ass? Damn right, he knows."

"Brain, how long you think it'll be before they come huntin' us?"

"We don't have to worry about the men left in the valley. But if their radios are still operational, they'll be calling across the river for help. Perhaps a day, two days at most."

"We could make it to the bridge in a day. Complete this mission and get the hell outta here."

Gunny overheard the conversation. "We could but we're stayin' put awhile longer. Charlie won't be expectin' that. If he sends reinforcements, we'll nail his dumb ass again."

"What about food, Sarge? We're about out."

"We'll get some dropped in when we head for the bridge."

Boots appeared out of the bushes at 1700 hours, right on schedule. She was rubbing up against their boots and mewing up a storm. Driggins gave her a piece of beef jerky he carried in his pack and she loved it. All Gonzales had was a C ration tin with those gooey lima beans and ham that tasted like grandmaw's homemade glue. He asked Henry to hold his rifle on him and make him eat it. They all laughed. He ate it, anyway.

That night the valley layered over with fog and they couldn't see squat. They heard movement but figured it was the leftovers from the air raid moving their wounded east toward the river. Red didn't play his radio. They were afraid of being spotted. Twenty-eight men against a large enemy force would be toast.

Next morning the fog was still there, so Gunny sent Red and Pasamenus with John and Bubba back down to recon what was going on underneath the stuff. They carried six canteens apiece tied together around their necks. That was easier than lugging them in two packs.

Bubba led them back through the trees, then east and down like Gunny had taught them. Never use the same trail twice. Down at the bottom of the hill they could see pretty well, even with the fog up above their heads. Everything was gray and misty with the overcast filtering out the sunlight. Beyond the trees, the elephant grass was ten feet high, so they used that for cover and made their way out to the waterway.

They came to a spot where the creek was sixteen or seventeen feet across, not real deep but it had fish in it. The elephant grass grew right up to the water's edge so they settled down in the greenery to wait and monitor the trail.

For three and a half hours they watched little water spiders scooting back and forth across the surface of the creek. Where their legs touched the surface, it looked like they were making dents in the water. They weren't really spiders at all but some kind of four-legged insect that glided around on the surface of ponds and creeks, same as back home.

When the sun finally got straight up, they proceeded to fill the canteens. They were almost finished when they looked up and there stood an old man with long white hair on the road right in front of them. The dude must have come out of the trees on the other side of the trail. He smiled and waved, then moved on. They waved back with that sick feeling one gets when trouble is brewing. Was he a friendly? Or one of those other jokers? They finished with the canteens, then cut back through the grass and trees and up the hillside.

"Yes, sir. He was old, white hair, wore a goatee like Uncle Ho. Raggedy clothes, no weapon. He wore sandals. No pack, just a walking stick. I'm sorry, lieutenant. I should have seen him first."

"That's all right, Smith. You got our water. Sergeant, assemble the men."

"Yes, sir."

Gunny went off into the trees to bring in the sentries. In a short while they were all assembled together on top of the hill.

"An old man spotted our water detail. We don't know if he's a friendly or sympathetic with Charlie. They probably know we're here because of that air strike last night. If the old man is one of theirs, they'll be on our case in a matter of hours. They must know we've been moving east because of the previous firefights. That's the negative part.

"Here's the positive. We've accomplished our mission. We can radio the choppers and get picked up down by the creek. That would be the smart thing to do. But the sergeant and I would like to try and hit them one more time before we abandon the area. So I'm leaving the decision up to you men. Sergeant Abernathy has suggested I pose the situation as part of your training, so listen up. Do we stay and continue east? Do we stay and reverse course? Or, do we pack up and go home?"

Quite a discussion took place. The majority of the men suggested they continue on toward the coast. Some said go back the way they came. A few wanted to call it a day and chopper out for a hot shower and meal. Then Pasamenus stood up and spoke.

"Sir, if I were the enemy commander, I would send out troops both east and west. That way they'll probably make contact, and they could catch us in an ambush. Why don't we cut across the valley and wait on the high ground, then if they show up again we can call down another air strike."

The men liked his idea, even the ones who had suggested returning to base. Gunny looked at the lieutenant and nodded his head. A vote was taken and the decision to stay in the area was made.

"You're a PFC, are you not?" The lieutenant had a friendly smile on his face.

"Yes, Sir, Private First Class Pasamanus, Sir."

"Consider yourself a buck sergeant from now on until we get back and I can fill out the paperwork. Sergeant Abernathy has a great deal of faith in this platoon, especially you, Pasamenus. It's been a pleasure serving with you men. Get 'em ready, sergeant."

"Sir, what about the cat?"

"Right, the cat…bring her with us."

They stuffed their gear into their field packs and got ready to move out. Gunny placed the cat in an empty pack they were using for C rations, fastening it up good so pussy would stay put. Then Lieutenant Butler led them down the side of the hill. Gunny brought up the rear with the kitty cat and his Thompson submachine gun. Bubba was out front with the M-60 gun, beside the lieutenant. Pasamenus was Tail-End Charlie with Gunny and Miss Boots.

It took nearly an hour for all of them to get across the valley floor and up the side of a steep-ass hill, which had as good a view on top as the one they just left. The sun was going down so Gunny posted sentries, then they formed a circle for chow. It was the last of the C rations. Boots got fed and the platoon settled down for the night.

"Sarge, can Red play his radio?"

"What do you think, lieutenant?

"No problem, just keep it down low."

Red turned it on and they listened to Saigon awhile. Country Joe & the Fish came on with "I-Feel-Like-I'm-Fixin'-To-Die," a song they had adopted back at Da Nang.

> *"And it's one, two, three,*
> *What are we fighting for?*
> *Don't ask me, I don't give a damn,*
> *Next stop is Vietnam;*
> *And it's five, six, seven,*
> *Open up the pearly gates,*
> *Well there ain't no time to wonder why,…"*

…then they all harmonized…

> *"Whoopee! We're all gonna die."*

"Lads, hold it down." But Gunny was laughing. So was Lieutenant Butler.

Then one of the sentries came in and motioned across the valley. Sarge and the lieutenant went to the edge and looked across. There were lights in the trees. They were searching for them. It wouldn't take them long to start across the valley once they found the place where the platoon had climbed down the hillside. Lieutenant Butler got on the horn and radioed their position.

"Affirmative, sir. They'll likely be crossing the valley floor in the next thirty to forty-five minutes. That's affirmative, colonel. We're on the opposite ridge from where we were last night. South side of the valley. Ask the flight leader to key me in once he's ready to make his bomb run."

They sat there waiting on pins and needles. They knew Charlie would be coming for them, which was what they had planned. Nevertheless, it seemed like hours, but the F-4s were there in thirty-nine minutes flat. Four jets came screaming by overhead, dropping flares over a long stretch of the valley. Then they saw them, nearly a hundred it looked like. The enemy troops began to run.

The first squadron came up the valley, four abreast, releasing their bombs dead on target. Shattering explosions, twenty-five or thirty of them right in a row. Then the second wave of Phantoms came roaring in four abreast. Another thundering barrage, smoke and debris flying in every direction. A third flight followed suit. They were beautiful, sleek, whup-ass machines. That accomplished, they came down two at a time, strafing with their 20 mm cannons while releasing the napalm. With the valley floor lit up in flames they made one final strafing pass, cutting down trees and men alike, then flew away for base.

Five men stood watch that night while the others slept. Every two hours they rotated. At 0400 hours a mortar round detonated in the hillside next to theirs. Then another round burst in the trees west of camp. The NVA didn't know exactly where the Marines were but they were searching. Another mortar shell exploded 100 yards east as the platoon gathered up their gear and headed off in that direction. They had just gotten out of camp when a round landed in the middle of where they'd been sleeping. The shelling continued intermittently, but by the time they'd covered half a mile it appeared they were out of harm's way, at least for the time being.

Traveling at night in a jungle is similar to walking inside a coal mine with the lights turned out. They couldn't see the man in front of them. So they stuck to the side of the ridge overlooking the valley as best they could. At least there they could see where they were going. Several times they had to detour back into the trees to get around another ledge or ravine. That's when one of the men tumbled down an embankment and buggered his wrist. Then somebody else got poked in the eye with a tree limb.

Finally, the lieutenant said to hell with it. They halted for the night and posted sentries, then hit the hay on the rim of the canyon. Dawn came early. They were up and moving at first light. All the food was gone but there was still coffee and cigarettes. Not bad fare for breakfast in the boondocks.

The North Vietnamese spotted the Marines crossing a bald spot on one of the hilltops, and they had yet to locate a place where the choppers could sit down and pick them up. The so-called plan was working a little too well. Mortars started coming again, so they went deeper into the jungle. The vegetation and vines got so thick in places that they got down on their hands and knees and crawled through them. The mosquitoes were terrible.

Finally, a helicopter arrived overhead, which was truly a blessed event. The men were elated to hear the friendly chatter of the chopper blades. They couldn't see him above the canopy of the trees, but they wanted to cheer, sing, boogie, break out the champagne. Instead, they kept their mouths shut for fear of getting shot. The pilot began directing them toward a clearing some 900 meters farther south. The evacuation helicopters were there and waiting. Meanwhile the A-1H pilots were circling overhead in case the Marines got into trouble.

About the time they were beginning to feel their piss and vinegar, an enemy force thirty yards back and to their left opened fire with AK-47s. Two dozen, it sounded like. They had been tracking Fourth Platoon all morning. The NVA commanders were royally pissed because the Marines had caused so much damage. The first volley caught Lieutenant Butler and Bubba in the legs. They couldn't see their antagonists, and Fourth Platoon was pinned down but good. Then another Marine got part of his hand shot off.

They returned fire, but things were going to go hell in a handbasket. They only carried so much ammunition, and the fighter bombers couldn't tell where they were in relation to the bad guys.

Gunny got on the radio asking the pilots to watch for tracers. Then he told Bubba to fire the M-60 machine gun straight up through the trees. It worked. A Skyraider laid down a spread of rockets across the enemy position. Gunny radioed a firing correction. Two more loosed a second and third barrage. Then another salvo, with Gunny directing the attack over their radio. A fifth A-1H dropped a pair of 500-pound bombs and that was all she wrote for those mothers.

The Marines bandaged up their wounded as best they could and moved out. Bubba and Lieutenant Butler could still walk but they were messed up. Gunny directed the Skyraiders into the trees up ahead, in case any surprises were waiting for them up there. It made walking easier with part of the undergrowth broken and blasted apart. Some of those plants were beautiful, with leaves as big around as those iron skillet monsters back at the mess hall. There were tall ferns and hanging vines with pink and red blossoms and little green and yellow butterflies fluttering about. The acrid stench from the munitions and the napalm hung in the thick jungle air, making their eyes water and their noses run.

Then another Kalashnikov started barking. They hit the deck, but one of them wasn't going home to visit mama ever again. John shot that bastard out of a tree, but a corporal was gut shot and had to be carried. Johnson hoisted him up on his shoulders and took off. The dead man's buddy sat there in those soggy, wet leaves, holding his lifeless hand and crying.

It brought back memories to Carlos of the time he saw a little girl drown at the swimming pool when he was a boy. Her father sat and held her hand and cried. Carlos had tears in his eyes. They were all brothers. Each loss took a piece of every one of them with it. The sad man stood up, handed his rifle to Carlos, gave his cartridge belt to another fellow, then picked up his dead friend in his arms. They moved out.

The lieutenant had lost so much blood it looked like he might have to be carried too. He kept stumbling but somehow managed to stay on his feet, using his M-14 as a cane. Bubba had the M-60 gun slung across his back, using a forked limb for a crutch. Gunny was leading them now, with Pasamenus bringing up the rear. They were still making decent progress, considering the jungle and the shape they were in, but a full company of North Vietnamese were in hot pursuit. Pasamenus could hear them signaling back and forth in the trees. He and Red kept up a running barrage behind them to hold the enemy at bay. Meanwhile, Fourth Platoon were dodging in and out behind evergreens and oak trees, passing M-14 magazines back as fast as they could dig them out of their bandoliers.

The jungle wasn't as thick here as what they had just passed through. Explosions began detonating close in on both sides, and some forty yards behind them, causing the ground to quake and the leaves to shower down from overhead. The Huey pilot radioed Gunny that more unwanted guests were arriving. The flyboys were blasting the jungle with missiles and 500-pound bombs trying to keep Charlie away, but of course, they couldn't see them all. The plan had worked to perfection, then backfired. Now they were running low on ammunition. Enemy gunfire began pouring out of the trees again. Chances of reaching the helicopters were looking more and more like even money. Bark and leaves were flying everywhere from the 7.62 rounds. Then another man got hit.

A canister of napalm exploded smack on their tails. It was terrifying and scalding hot. Pasamenus and Red felt the searing heat. Then they heard that awful screaming again. Then another A-1H dropped two more canisters, and more screaming. Enemy fire was coming from everywhere. They were up Shit Creek in Shit City. It sounded like the whole North Vietnamese Army was coming through the jungle right behind them.

Enemy mortar rounds started banging away off to their right. Charlie was walking them into the column. A mortar shell came whistling down and burst in the branches directly above their heads. It wounded several of the men around Gonzales. He caught a piece in the neck. It wasn't serious but it hurt, like getting stung by one of those big orange wasps. It was a 120 mm and Charlie had the range. Two of the Skyraiders roared away, going after the gun crew. Gunny kept the radioman beside him the whole time, urging the men forward as fast as the wounded could manage. Then another round came crashing down striking a Marine dead center, right in front of Henry. It blew him all over the trees. There was nothing left but his M-14 rifle and his leather boots. His feet were still inside, and part of his legs from the crotch down.

"This way, Marines. Follow me!"

They veered off to their right with Gunny breaking the trail. The undergrowth there was sparse and mostly open. Then they cut back south at a slow trot. Lieutenant Butler fell down, but John and Driggins got him up on his feet and they continued on. Johnson was huffing and puffing and sweating like a cold beer left out in the noonday sun, but he was doing fine with the wounded corporal.

Commie mortar bursts were behind them now. The Marine carrying his dead buddy collapsed and sprawled in the leaves, so two more

Marines took the limp body between them, dragging it by the wrists. The man they relieved was exhausted and covered with the blood of his dead friend. John and Carlos stopped a few moments to let him catch his breath. Gunny came running back to see what the holdup was. When he found them, he motioned the others to go on while he waited. Red and Pasamenus came in through the trees and waited there with them.

It was a proud moment, and humble too, to be in the presence of such brave and courageous men. They were all scared. Nobody is immune when the bullets start cracking and whining, but they worked together as a team of professional warriors and Marine Corps brothers. It is a tradition of the Marine Corps never to leave a dead man behind if at all possible. They were fulfilling that tradition in the jungles of Vietnam, with death dogging their heels every step they took.

All manner of hell began breaking loose behind them. The A-1s were plastering the jungle with everything they had. Up ahead they could hear the familiar whomp-whomp-whomp of the helicopter blades. They were almost there. High above them they heard the welcome drone of a new squadron of Skyraiders. Carlos was so relieved he started to laugh. He laughed so hard it hurt because of the shrapnel in his neck. Maybe he was goofy from losing blood. Gunny looked at Carlos and he began laughing too. Deliverance was at hand. They broke into the clearing and ran for the choppers.

With Gunny directing the withdrawal they loaded up the first two helicopters with six men apiece and sent them on their way. Most of the wounded went with them. The next chopper took Johnson and his damaged cargo, plus another Marine carrying the dead man, and his worn-out buddy. They tossed in the extra weapons, their gear, an extra radio, and those boots with the man's legs inside, which Henry had wrapped up inside two field packs. Eighteen down and ten to go.

The fourth helicopter was loaded with only three men. It had been hit by ground fire and Gunny didn't want to chance overheating the engine. The machine was backfiring, but otherwise appeared to be running smoothly. The pilot sat there, waiting for the rest of them to get loaded aboard the last Huey. His door gunner and the other door gunner were a matched set. Brothers out of Junction City, Kansas.

Gunny was helping the lieutenant climb onboard when something knocked the breath out of Carlos and he fell flat of his back. It was true what they said about slow motion. He could hear gunfire, but it sounded miles away…and everyone was moving like one of those picture shows where they slow down the characters to quarter speed…the door gunner was firing into the jungle directly above his head…he watched the spent cartridge casings floating down, bouncing about on the ground.

Red came running across the field from the other chopper with a machine gun in his hands. He had run over there when he saw Gunny was in trouble…enemy bullets knocked Red tumbling to the ground, but he staggered back up and kept on running. Gunny tossed the cat satchel to Butler…Carlos watched her float through the air. Then Gunny turned around slowly to say something to Bubba…the Thompson fell from his hands and he collapsed in the grass…green tracers were pouring out of the trees…Bubba opened fire with the M-60 gun…Pasamenus and John began empting the last of their magazines…Carlos watched the empty clips floating down as they reloaded.

The pilot was screaming, "GET IN! GET IN !"

John flung his weapon onboard, loaded Gunny, then he picked Carlos up and threw him inside. It was true, as well, about men having super strength during times of peril…Bubba hobbled onboard…both door gunners were blasting nonstop, pounding the tree line where an enemy machine gun was kicking their ass…Pasamanus clamored in…John was standing in the doorway, firing Bubba's M-60 beside the door gunner. Red was lying on the floor between their legs firing his machine gun…more green tracers, striking the door gunner and

John…pieces of the helicopter flew off the walls…John lost the M-60 out the door as they were lifting off, falling over backwards on top of the master sergeant. The wounded doorman was lying beside them, tethered to the chopper by a safety line.

It was all so strange and so terribly slow. Carlos looked into John's eyes, where they lay together on the blood-smeared floor, as John's complexion bled away to a whiter shade of pale. John…please don't go…he reached over and held his brother's hand…we made it…we're going home.

John stared at Carlos with a bewildered expression on his face… then he gazed over at Bubba…whispered Samantha's name…and he was gone.

Bubba was sobbing and pounding the deck with is fists… Pasamenus had that 1,000 yard stare from battle fatigue…Red was cursing and beating the side of the helicopter like a mad man.

Gunny was shot through and through…blood was everywhere…it occurred then to Carlos that he might be dying…he wanted to cry too, but couldn't remember how…John's eyes had turned the color of faded denim. Then Carlos fell down a long, empty kaleidoscope…there was no feeling in his hands…he could smell the napalm burning…and hear Madame Mimi's girlish laughter…and the Whomp-Whomp-Whomp of the helicopter blades.

Chapter Thirty-Three

The School Yard

A little boy stood in the middle of a barren schoolyard beside an empty merry-go-round they pushed to make go in circles, then jumped onboard and rode the thing. He was alone. A short distance away stood an empty set of swings where he and his chums used to push one another and swing up a storm during recess.

Over by a wooden fence for the farmer's cows was the playground where they played softball, skipped rope, and chased one another playing tag. Baked red clay, a small pitcher's mound, and four dusty bases for running, hooting, and hollering. Behind the playground stood an array of tall oak trees. Back in the trees some fifty yards sat Mister Horne's house, which faced out on Taylor Road. His friend Charlie lived there.

He was reflecting on the time when Mister Horne dug a drain field out back for his new residence. The trench sat open for several months while the house was being built. The rains came and filled up the hole with water. He and Charlie had marvelous times back there, catching bullfrogs attracted by the pond. That was their special world when hop toads were everywhere, tiny glowworms lit up the fields at night, and salamanders lived in the creek down behind his parents' house on Royal Heights Drive.

Tears slid down his little face. A new school ordinance decreed that he must leave his cherished Galbraith Elementary, due to an overcrowding condition, and attend Mooreland Heights on the other side of Chapman Highway. He had attempted to slip through that very morning, riding his old school bus to Galbraith, but the fifth-grade teacher had turned him away, telling him he must obey the rules.

Frightened and confused, he was sent to the principal's office where he asked the principal to call his daddy to come pick him up. Now he waited on the edge of the merry-go-round, his heart breaking in pieces, tears leaking down his cheeks, falling to the dusty ground below forming tiny damp circles between his Buster Brown shoes.

The door was closing on his old world. A new door was about to open.

A long, black limousine swung around the corner off Taylor Road onto Galbraith School Road, stopping beside the playground across from the little boy, and sat there with the motor running. The child hesitated, uncertain. Thinking it might be his father, he got up and walked across the playground to the shining black automobile. He opened the door on the passenger side and looked in.

"Get in, son." The friendly voice sounded familiar.

He did as he was told, climbed up on the running board, then settled himself inside on the front seat. The driver reached across the little boy, pulling the car door shut with a final thump.

Then something wonderful happened. The sad little boy transformed into John the man, a United States Marine. Gunny Sergeant Abernathy was driving. They were wearing their dress blue uniforms. Other Marines sat in the back seat, but John didn't look back there. He sat gazing at the driver.

"Where's my daddy?" he asked.

"Your father isn't coming. They sent me in his place."

"But why? I don't understand. I have to change schools."

"School days are over, son. You're a man now."

"I remember you. We were in the war together."

"You were a good soldier, John. One of the best."

"Where's Sam? Where's my wife?"

"Samantha will join you in good time. Right now she has other matters to attend to."

"Where's Bubba? Where's the rest of the men?"

"Robert Smith is in the hospital in Da Nang. He and Lieutenant Butler are on the same floor together. Gonzales and Red are there with them. Pasamenus made sergeant. Johnson is a corporal now. Your friend Red won the silver star for heroism. Pasamenus and Driggins both received bronze stars."

"What about Henry and Sophie? What about Madame?"

"The Henrys are doing well. Mimi is a trooper. She'll be living in Paris soon."

"Do you miss her?"

"I miss that woman with all my heart. She'll be along one of these days."

"But what are we doing here? I don't understand."

"You have a journey to make. To a wonderful new home."

"Is it far?"

"It's a long ways, John. But I'm coming with you."

"I think I understand now. Are my parents all right?"

"They're hurt and upset, but they'll be along before you know it."

"Will Sam be very long?"

"Your wife has cancer, John. Her doctors just found out."

"Will she suffer much?"

"Some, but that will end soon. Then you'll be together again."

A golden shaft of sunlight shown down on the limousine from a beautiful cloudless blue sky. John knew it was time to go. He turned to look out the window one last time at his old grammar school playground. John had spent four happy years there. Sweet, innocent years of a happy, carefree childhood. He was amazed to see so many children standing outside the limousine window. They filled the playground, back beneath the oak trees, sitting on the swings, the merry-go-round, the schoolhouse steps. There were little Vietnamese boys and girls, Korean and Chinese youngsters, French, Australian, little American children, German and Russian. Then he saw that their numbers stretched all the way into the hills where the sky was turning brilliant hues of purple and orange. Sad little boys and girls. And each one appeared to be waiting for something.

Tears filled his eyes. "What does it mean, Gunny? Why are those children out there?"

"Those are the casualties of war, John. They're waiting for someone to come pick them up. A mother, a father, somebody like me, perhaps."

"Somebody to come take them away?"

"Yes."

"Will they be happy then?"

"They'll be happy the rest of their lives."

"But where will they go, Sarge? What happens when they leave the playground?"

"They're going home, son. We're all going home."

This is not the End. It is just the Beginning.

LITTLE BOY BLUE

The little toy dog is covered with dust,
But sturdy and staunch he stands;
And the little toy soldier is red with rust,
And his musket molds in his hands.
Time was when the little toy dog was new,
And the soldier was passing fair;
And that was the time when our Little Boy Blue
Kissed them and put them there.

"Now don't you go till I come," he said,
"And don't you make any noise!"
So, toddling off to his trundle-bed,
He dreamt of the pretty toys;
And, as he was dreaming, an angel song
Awakened our Little Boy Blue—
Oh! the years are many, the years are long,
But the little toy friends are true!

Ay, faithful to Little Boy Blue they stand,
Each in the same old place—
Awaiting the touch of a little hand,
The smile of a little face;
And they wonder, as waiting the long years
through
In the dust of that little chair,
What has become of our Little Boy Blue,
Since he kissed them and put them there.

Eugene Field

Mister Jackson (lower right), his friends, and John.

Acknowledgments

Special thanks to Roland Clare for his assistance in connecting me with Keith Reid of Procol Harum in England. Joe McDonald with Country Joe & The Fish gave his blessing from California. I want to thank the Morton family in Knoxville, TN. Freddie Morton ran The Down Under nightclub when I was a young man. Freddie is now with God. Thanks to John Lockridge for allowing me to use his name with his Southern parody about the Old South. Susan Preston is another dear friend from that long ago era of carefree days and fabulous music.

Dan Butler served three tours in Vietnam. Dan is my cousin who helped out with dates and locations in Vietnam. Colonel Butler is a brave and courageous individual. I wish to acknowledge my sister Judy Henry for proof reading the tale. Several of her comments were added, most notably "the fat lady had just sung." Thanks to the Lawson McGee Library in Knoxville, who assisted with spelling, and Betty Davis in Atlanta for sharing her knowledge of French. And Becky Henry, my second sister in Miami, who always told me I should write a book someday.

Thanks to the Magbee Brothers Lumber Company in Georgia for letting me use Fletcher's name. I worked at his lumber company 40 years ago in Norcross, GA. My friend Fletcher Magbee is deceased. Thank you Doris Sams for ok'ing Bob Sams, her father, for one of my characters. He was best friends with my father, Jay Henry.

Bob and Jay are gone now, but Doris lives on over in Vestal where I was born. She pitched and played outfield in that real life drama, *A League Of Their Own*.

A very special thank you to Jamie Saloff who formatted *Garden of Eden*. Jamie steered me through the minefields of my own literary mistakes. And Sharon Garner for editing, and Cory Mullenhour for his wonderful art work. Tom Bird, author and lecturer, referred me to Jamie.

Young High School and the Southern Circle are only memories now, and being young once, and full of life and adventure. I miss those glory days, but Vietnam was a politically-induced tragedy. Four and a half million Vietnamese perished, and 58,156 Americans.

Last of all, I wish to say thanks to all the people I've known and loved along the trail who gave me the ability to see beyond my own back yard. I stubbed my toe a time or two, but it's been a hell of a journey. My apologies to anyone I overlooked.

God bless each and every one of you,

Larry Jay Henry
Louisville, Tennessee

Contact the Author

To Contact the Author, visit his website at:

McAnallyFlatsPress.com

Or write to him via the publisher at:

McAnally Flats Press
PO Box 1058
Louisville, TN 37777

LaVergne, TN USA
28 December 2009
168193LV00001B/6/P

9 780981 920900